Desert Destiny

Book 7
The Wolves of Twin Moon Ranch

Anna Lowe

Contents

Free Books

Get your free e-books now!

Sign up for my newsletter at *annalowebooks.com* to get three free books!

- *Desert Wolf*: Friend or Foe (Book 1.1 in the Twin Moon Ranch series)

- *Off the Charts* (the prequel to the Serendipity Adventure series)

- *Perfection* (the prequel to the Blue Moon Saloon series)

Author's Note

This story was written years after the rest of the *Twin Moon* and *Blue Moon Saloon* series, and it takes place after the events of those books. So, the timeline is a little unusual in that way, but don't worry — *Desert Destiny* can be read as a stand-alone story, and it doesn't contain any spoilers for the *Blue Moon Saloon* series. You can just enjoy it for itself and as another chance to connect with a unique and close-knit wolf pack in a beautiful part of the world. Happy reading!

Chapter One

"So, how many skinwalkers did you arrest today?"

Andie closed the door of her squad car and headed for headquarters, ignoring Chavez. "No such thing, remember?"

Chavez tsked. "Officer Hale, haven't you spent enough time in Arizona to know the legends are true?"

"Apparently not." She strode on, paying more attention to her surroundings than to Chavez. The beauty of northern Arizona never ceased to awe her, even after another long, tough day at work. Snow dusted the pine trees on the hills around town, and the setting sun cast rocky red outcrops into an even richer hue.

Her partner, Kyle, did the same, flaring his nostrils and closing his eyes. A moment later, a tiny smile played over his lips, probably as he anticipated going home to his wife and kids.

A month ago, that would have made Andie sigh and yearn. But now, her heart beat a little faster, because Kyle wasn't the only one with a special someone to head home to.

She hid a smile before someone caught it — like Lee or, worse, Chavez, whose duty shifts ended the same time as hers.

"How was your day, Lee?" Andie asked Chavez's partner. "All good?"

"Well, considering we spent the day looking for a giant chicken..." Chavez butted in.

"Cassowary," Lee corrected.

"Whatever. A really big, really dangerous chicken with talons as long as my finger — or other body parts."

"That small, huh?" Andie quipped.

Everyone burst into laughter, and even Chavez grinned.

"Good one, Hale. Good one. The main thing is, I've survived the day — and another twelve-hour shift with this clown." He pointed to his partner.

Lee snickered. "Yeah, yeah. Just remember who's covering your ass next time things heat up."

"That's the thing. Maybe you should be the one to go ahead while I cover your ass," Chavez shot back. "Or, wait. Forget that. I'm not sure I can handle the view." Then he turned and bumped Kyle. "I know. You and I can swap partners." He waggled his eyebrows at Andie. "Now that would be a view."

Andie sighed inwardly, having heard it all before. One of the guys had once stuck a picture of Cindy Crawford on her locker, claiming a close resemblance. As if. Andie might have the same chestnut hair, trim figure, and long legs, but she had better things to do than prance along catwalks in high heels — a point she'd emphasized by replacing that photo with a classic Western movie still of a young Clint Eastwood, coolly lighting a stick of dynamite with his cigar. That was the image she preferred. Tough. Unflappable. Smart. Someone you didn't mess with, or else.

She shot Chavez a killer look and turned to Kyle. "Remind me again — what's the procedure for booking a cop on sexual harassment?"

Chavez cackled. "Ha. Gotcha. I meant I get Kyle. You and me, big guy." He put a hand on Kyle's shoulder. "What do you think?"

Kyle shrugged him off. "Not happening, Chavez."

"Damn." Lee sighed, holding the door to headquarters open. "I keep hoping to get rid of this yo-yo."

Chavez rolled his eyes and led the way in, keeping up a constant stream of chatter as they went about their end-of-shift routines — turning in their gear, signing off on the day's reports, and trading uniform jackets for civilian wear that was less conspicuous for travel home.

"Don't spend too long fixing your hair, Hale," Chavez joked as Andie sped through her routine.

Andie ignored him, like she often ignored her mother. The woman was always nagging her to get a new hairdo, a new job, and a new man — any man, as far as her mother was concerned.

"Don't spend too much on yours," she shot back, sweeping a hand over his bald head.

He grinned. "Are you kidding? The ladies can't get enough of me this way."

"Ladies? Plural?" Lee laughed. "One would be a good start, man."

Chavez made a face then laughed at the newspaper lying in the locker room.

"Ha. Did you see this? We made national news." Chavez held up the front page as Andie pulled on the worn bomber jacket that had once been her dad's.

She glanced over, then rolled her eyes. "If you call that trashy paper news."

Skinwalker sighted! the headline screamed over a sketch of a man clad in a wolf's pelt.

"Great." Lee shook his head. "Now we'll have every nutcase who believes in that crap coming through town."

Andie sighed. "Sometimes I think we already do."

"Could be worse. Could be Sedona." Chavez mimicked a spiritual pose. "The vortex! I feel the power of the vortex!"

Lee made a face. "True."

"Oh. Oh! We can ask that neighbor of yours," Chavez went on. "She claims to have seen a skinwalker, right?"

Andie nodded wearily. Yvette, a fiftysomething bohemian artist type, was definitely one of a kind.

"Yep. She claims to have seen it four times — but this is also the woman who reported seeing human footprints morphing seamlessly into bear tracks up in the woods. The same woman who claims to have heard a hellhound around town. Remember that, a few years back?"

She glanced at Kyle, but he remained silent and expressionless.

"Maybe she's right," Chavez tried.

"And maybe I'll win the state lottery tonight," Lee observed.

"If she's seen anything, it's just a couple of kids playing pranks," Andie pointed out. "That or someone trying to scare off buyers for Lazy Q Ranch."

Hundreds of acres of land to the east of town were up for sale, and developers were moving in fast.

There must be some way to stop those big-city jerks, Yvette had said.

Andie's heart panged, thinking of all the beauty and wildlife that would be destroyed.

And just like that, the homeward pull intensified. She grabbed her keys and headed for the door.

"Wow. Someone's in a rush tonight," Chavez teased. "Got a hot date?"

Andie waved goodbye without saying a word. Not exactly a hot date. But she did have special company to look forward to that night.

Chapter Two

On the drive home, Andie finger-combed her long, chestnut hair out of the tight bun she used for work, then craned her neck to glance at the stars. Gradually, the dense streets of the city center gave way to the wide boulevards of surrounding strip malls. Then those petered out too, leaving her with the open panorama she loved.

Northern Arizona. All that raw, rugged beauty and solitude. No one out there but her and that jackrabbit bounding across the road, its oversized ears on high alert. Bats flitted around the cottonwoods that followed the curving path of a creek. Overhead, a universe of stars glittered and winked.

God, she loved the high-altitude desert. The delicate details, the grand mesas. The subtle seasons. Especially her little corner of paradise, down on a bumpy dirt track well out of town.

The road rose to a viewpoint overlooking Lazy Q Ranch. A cluster of bright lights marked the old homestead at the heart of the ranch. Dimmer necklaces of light branched out from there, outlining sheds, paddocks, and stock pens.

Otherwise, there was just open, undulating range, apart from three scattered dots of light — one for each of the smaller properties around the ranch. The goatherd lived in the old bunkhouse over to the west. Yvette, the artist, occupied a converted smokehouse, way over to the east. Andie rented the third place — a little cottage built for the ranch manager nearly a century ago. She took a hard right onto a half-mile-long track that served as her driveway, then hit the brakes.

"Howdy, neighbors," she murmured at the fifty-plus goats blocking her way.

They trotted across the road, bleating as they went. Andie rolled down the window, letting in chilly night air along with the cacophony of their clanging bells.

"Hiya, Jose," she called to the goatherd. "You're out late tonight."

He tipped his hat from the saddle of Chico, his palomino.

"*Sí.* Four goats wandered off, and it took an hour to round them all up again."

One of Jose's Pyrenean mountain dogs put its front paws on the running board of Andie's truck and stuck its muzzle in the window.

Andie laughed and petted it between the ears. "Hiya, Lucky. Are you a good dog?"

Jose shook his head. "No. He let the goats wander off."

Andie rubbed harder, whispering, "You're still a good dog."

Lucky leaned into her hand, then reluctantly stepped away at Jose's command.

"*Vamanos.* Time to go home. *Hasta luego, amiga.*"

Andie waved and waited for the last goat to pass. Then she eased into gear and covered the remaining distance to her place. Solar garden lights outlined the walkway, providing just enough illumination to fit her key into the lock. Yes, an actual lock, even way out here where no thief would wander. Yvette laughed at that, but hey. Between growing up in California and working in law enforcement, Andie hadn't been able to shake the habit.

On the drive home, her energy had flagged. But now, anticipation made her hurry through the house. Grabbing a container of the previous night's leftovers, she stepped across the back porch and down three crooked stairs. Then she ducked under the laundry line and crossed the worn patch of ground that passed for a yard. Finally, she crested a rise and jumped onto a flat-topped throne of a rock. There, she stood, taking it all in.

All that space. All those stars. All there for her to soak in like a dream.

Once upon a time, the stars were her main attraction, but nowadays, she leveled her gaze at the ground.

"Are you out there, buddy?" Her heart skipped as she whispered into the night.

The bushes stirred, but it was only the wind.

She stood for one long, hopeful minute, then sank down to wait. To hope. To dream. She ate quickly, then sat with her knees pulled up to her chest and her chin on her arms, replaying the good and bad of the day. Then a soft chuff sounded, and she snapped up her head.

"There you are." She burst into a grin. "Good to see you!"

An understatement, really, because her heart revved, and her spirit soared. Every time she saw her friend, childlike joy swept over her, and she smiled so broadly, her cheeks ached. Funny, what effect one canine could have on a girl.

Then again, it wasn't every girl who had a wild wolf drop in to visit now and then.

Yes, a wolf. Not a coyote, as she'd thought the first time she'd spotted him pacing the perimeter of her place. An honest to God, grayish-brown wolf she'd taken to calling Buck, after the canine hero of *The Call of the Wild,* her childhood idol.

He chuffed again, and her mind translated the words.

Good to see you too. How are you doing tonight?

"Doing good now," she whispered. "How about you? Everything okay?"

He flicked his ears and wagged his tail as if to say, *Doing fine, thanks.*

Most folks would think her crazy to get so close to a wild animal — or to imagine communicating with one — but Buck was special that way. At first, he'd been a mere shadow, crouched low in the darkness, watching her. More of a presence, really, than something she could pick out from the landscape. Then, over the course of six weeks, he'd started pacing carefully into sight, closer and closer until—

Andie's breath caught as Buck strode right up to the foot of her rock with none of the wariness he'd shown the first time. On the contrary, he looked as happy to see her as she was to see him.

"Sorry I missed you yesterday," she whispered. "Work kept me late."

His tail drooped slightly, then wagged harder, forgiving her.

She grinned, then caught herself reaching out to pet him. Quickly, she drew her hand back. Buck was a wild animal, and she'd sworn not to touch, feed, or approach him. She'd already bent those rules in letting Buck approach her, but she had to stand firm on the rest for his own protection. Wild animals couldn't tell the difference between friendly humans and trigger-happy hunters.

Of course, giving him a name was probably a bad idea, but she couldn't help that either.

Buck, as in The Call of the Wild, *she'd told him one night, early on. Would you mind if I called you that?*

He didn't seem to mind. And silly her, she'd even gone as far as introducing herself.

I'm Andie. Well, Andrea. Pleased to meet you, Buck.

As if a wild animal cared.

But that was the funny thing with Buck. He was so sharp and attentive, it seemed he truly did care.

They sat in amiable silence for a few minutes, listening to the sounds of the desert at night. The rustle of grass in the light breeze, the fleeting twitch of insects. The faint scent of spruce wafting over from the mountains.

"Not too cold for you last night?" she asked quietly.

Buck's eyes flashed as if to say, *Cold? Me?*

She chuckled, picturing him talking in a cowboy drawl, because if Buck were a person, that's what he would be. One of those tall, quiet, square-jawed guys who shook off everything from bad weather to bad luck. All humility, wiry muscle, and heart.

Funny, how gazing into those deep, soulful eyes made her imagination go wild.

Then she gave herself a little shake and nodded to Buck. "I guess you never really get cold. You have the perfect coat."

It really was — thick and healthy, with dark browns and deep grays that went black at his extremities.

He looked at her expectantly until she crossed her arms over her jacket. "I'm fine. This is my dad's jacket, you know."

When he cocked his head, she ran a hand along the fleece collar. "When I was a kid, he always talked about growing up in Arizona and how beautiful the night sky was here. So, I finally moved out here to see for myself."

A familiar lump formed in her throat as she looked up. The Big Dipper lined up directly before her, pointing to the North Star. Orion, the hunter, strode through the celestial landscape with Sirius at his heels, while way over to the south, Scorpio sliced the sky with his curved tail.

"Beautiful," she murmured, wishing her dad could see her now.

Far off in the distance, a truck wound in and out of sight, more a set of jumpy lights than sound. Andie winced, imagining cement trucks smothering the soil. Sometime soon, they would, because Lazy Q Ranch was for sale, and developers were moving in. Eventually, grazing livestock would be replaced by sleek SUVs, and fences would carve the vast landscape into tiny parcels. This corner of Arizona would be ruined forever. What would become of Buck then?

She rested her chin on her knees, gazing at him.

When he cocked his head, she didn't have the heart to voice her concerns. Instead, she mumbled, "Sorry. It's just that people suck sometimes."

Funny, how his eyes flickered as if to say, *You can say that again.*

"Still, it's a beautiful night," she whispered, forcing glum thoughts away.

Buck looked around, then gave himself a little shake and circled her boulder twice. Then he settled down near her feet, gazing in the same direction as she. That was a little ritual Buck had developed, much to her delight. Circling her, inspecting the area, then settling in like a king studying his realm.

And there they sat, like a pair of old friends. Friends who didn't have to speak to be understood. Friends who valued the same things and loved the wilderness in exactly the same way. The kind of friend she had never found in the human world and probably never would.

Joy and melancholy bubbled side by side, but she pushed the latter away.

"A beautiful night," she whispered.

Buck flicked his ears, and she imagined his reply. *A beautiful night, indeed.*

Chapter Three

Roy closed his eyes, sniffed the air, and took a deep breath. It truly was a beautiful night. He had everything he needed. A full stomach, thanks to a successful hunt earlier that day. Comfortable body temperature, too — chilly on top, where his fur protected him, and warm below, with the rocks radiating heat absorbed during the day. What else did a wolf shifter need?

Nothing, really. Nothing but space. Silence. Serenity. Those were harder to find sometimes, but they always seemed to be floating around Andie.

My nice lady, the canine part of his mind sighed happily.

Friend, the dreamy, human part corrected.

Mate, the deepest part of his soul rumbled.

At times like these, when life seemed so perfect, he didn't bother to differentiate between all those. She was his, and he was hers. Simple as could be.

That was the good thing about living as a wolf for so long. Everything was so much simpler that way.

He flicked an ear, listening to her steady breath and the rustle of her clothes. That outer layer she wore was a funny thing. It had a narrow collar of fur but smelled of cow, yet she seemed perfectly at ease wrapping herself in that scent.

Not cow. Leather, a distant corner of his mind said.

He wrinkled his nose, focusing on Andie's scent. There it was — sweet and special, like the flower of a prickly pear. The kind of scent you only caught a whiff of now and then, when the flowers first opened after a long time locked away.

A little like Andie. Locked up tightly, only allowing tiny glimpses of the beauty within. Of course, part of him thrilled at her outer beauty too. The fine curve of her eyebrows. The perfect line of her lips. The smooth, high cheeks. Her light, athletic curves. And best of all, those green-brown eyes that shone at the stars... and at him.

He inhaled, getting his fill of the idyllic night. Not even the light she left on in the house bothered him. It was soft, like her voice. And truthfully, he liked a lot of things about her place. The way it stood on its own, without a dozen other houses, vehicles, or noisy machines. The tempting scents that came from the kitchen, the squeak of the screen door that signaled her comings and goings... All in all, a place he could get used to.

So much, it made something in him yearn for the home he'd once known. A comfortable place, with food at the ready and water on demand. Blankets in the winter, shade in the summer, all in one place, without the need to roam, fight, or defend. A place he could let down his guard.

Then he gave himself a shake. This was as close as he would let himself get to a house or a person ever again. He didn't need or want any part of the human world.

But this woman...

She was so different. So special. So easy to picture out in the desert in wolf form, enjoying the vast world with him.

"Did you have a good day?" she asked.

Most humans barked, yelled, or squeaked. But Andie had a softer manner of speaking. Singing, almost, very gently, like a lullaby.

Lullaby... A distant memory flitted through his mind, along with a woman's voice. Just as quickly as it came, it left, though a warm feeling remained.

He raised his head, eager to please Andie. Had he had a good day?

He thought it over, then frowned. Wolf memories weren't like human ones that flowed like a river from beginning to end. They were more like clouds that wafted back and forth on a breeze, clustered by category rather than space or time. Memories of pain. Memories of anger. Good tastes, bad tastes. Dark places, bright places. Hot. Cold.

So, it was hard to say. Even if he thought hard, there were little gaps where time had left no trace. All totally normal for a wolf who focused on the present rather than the future or past, and who didn't torture himself with thoughts every minute of every day.

He strained to remember for a while, then let his tail thump a few times. It was a good day now, right?

When Andie chuckled, his tail thumped harder, and a warm sensation filled his soul.

"You know the best part of my day?" she asked.

He held his breath, waiting.

"This," she whispered.

He wagged his tail. *Same for me.*

She was the highlight of his day, every day. Or at least, the times she was there. Some nights, she didn't return home until really late or after he'd had to move along.

That was one thing he forced himself to do — move on. The longer he stayed in one place, the harder it was to leave, and the more likely that he would stumble across shifters he would rather avoid.

A faraway rumble registered in the earth, and he flicked an ear. A moment later, he jumped to his feet and studied the road.

Andie jumped down from the boulder too. "What is it?"

A vehicle appeared in the distance, sending up a plume of dust. Painfully bright red-and-blue lights flashed from the roof, making him squint.

Andie cussed from his side. "Shoot. Something's going on at the ranch."

Roy recoiled when the vehicle rattled over a bump, then halted as a pleasant tingle went through his side. He glanced up. Wait. Had Andie gently brushed his back, telling him it would be okay?

For weeks, he'd burned for her touch. And, wow. It was as nice as he'd dreamed. Really nice, like lapping cool water from a shady stream on a blistering day.

Too bad it was happening now, with instinct telling him to run. He took another skittish step back, watching the road.

"Just one squad car," Andie observed, though her voice was tense.

Together, they watched the vehicle turn toward the heart of Lazy Q Ranch, half a mile away.

Roy paced, torn between staying at her side and escaping those piercing lights. Just one car? That was like "just" one beehive, the way it exploded and took over the night.

"Damn." Andie stepped toward her driveway, then turned back to explain. "I'd better go see what's going on."

He stared. Go? She wanted to purposely head into that chaos instead of away?

I don't want you to go, he burned to say. *I never want you to leave.*

But that was the shitty thing about life sometimes. What you wanted and what you got were two different things.

"It will be fine," she assured him. "I'll see you soon, all right?"

No, it wasn't all right. Not when he knew how unpredictably dangerous humans could be.

Andie took another step, looking as torn as he felt. "You take care, okay?"

He nearly snorted. The desert was safe and secure. If nothing else, it operated according to natural laws. It was the human world that was all fucked up.

He let out a low whine. *You're the one who has to take care. Please.*

The screen door squeaked when Andie opened it, and she paused halfway in, as if she didn't really want to go.

So, don't, he wanted to bark. *Stay with me. Come out to the desert and life a quieter, simpler life.*

And just like that, his mind took off with a dozen fantasies of the wonderful life they could share. Even the corner of his mind that said, *She can't. She's not a shifter,* didn't really register at first.

By the time he'd blinked his way out of that disorienting daze, Andie was moving into the house.

"Take care, Buck. See you soon."

Would she? Would he? How did she know?

Moments later, her front door slammed, followed by the roar of her truck coming to life. By the time his heart hit its next, worried beat, Andie had reversed out of the drive and sped down the road.

Chapter Four

Andie glanced in the rearview mirror. Leaving Buck was always hard, but it seemed harder each time, as if a little shred of her soul tore away to stay with him.

Still, there was no ignoring the urgency in that squad car. So she fired up her pickup and sped down the road. A half-mile later, she turned under the gate of the Lazy Q Ranch and coasted to a stop under the barn floodlights. Stepping out of her vehicle, she greeted Officers Hanson and Arivera with a nod. The latter broke away from a cluster of people to meet her.

"Officer Hale. Too bad this call didn't come in two hours ago." He kept his voice low despite the background noise of barking dogs. "You would have had the pleasure of taking a report from the lovely Mr. Brady — and your nosy neighbor, Ms. Witt." He chuckled at Andie's reaction. "Surprised she beat you over when there might be gossip involved?"

Andie sighed. That was Yvette, all right.

"What happened?"

Arivera grimaced. "Come see for yourself."

The moment Andie stepped toward the paddock, a red-faced man stopped hollering at the others and glared. "You."

She gave him a cool nod. "Mr. Brady."

He huffed. "Some good having a cop in the neighborhood is. Where the hell were you?"

Hanson stuck up the tablet he had been typing into. "Let's stay focused on the report, sir. You said you returned to the ranch at about nine?"

Brady whipped around like an angry bull. "What's the matter? You deaf? Yes, I came back at nine and saw that."

Andie followed his gesture to the paddock, where a dozen steer stood. They were the last of a herd of hundreds, most of which had been sold along with many other assets. One of the steer leaned against the fence, its sides heaving and eyes wide.

"Whoa, there. Whoa, now." One of the ranch hands inched closer.

The movement gave Andie a clearer view of the steer's bloodstained flank. With a little gasp, she peered closer, along with everyone else.

"That there's our best steer of the season, and he's slit half open," Brady raged.

Brady had only been around for a few months, but Andie was already familiar with his blustery outbreaks. Still, he wasn't exaggerating for once. The steer's side was sliced by two long, parallel marks.

"Have you called the vet?" she asked.

Arivera nodded, but that just set Brady off on another tirade. "The vet? Little good he'll do now."

"She," Hansen noted quietly. "Dr. Lucas is a she."

Brady turned a deeper shade of crimson. "Even worse. Anyway, that steer's as good as dead."

"Actually, it looks worse than it is," the ranch hand started, then trailed off at Brady's murderous glare.

Andie shot Brady a look. Did he actually want the poor beast to die? It sure seemed like it.

And boy, had times changed. For decades, Lazy Q Ranch had been managed by ranchers who went back five generations on that very land. But the ranch owners had recently passed away, and their heirs made no secret of cashing in on the land. Brady was a new hire, brought in to maximize profits, including subdividing the land. A steer here or there wasn't his concern — unless it figured into a profitable insurance claim.

"Now, you tell me. What the hell did that to my steer?" Brady demanded.

"Skinwalker," Yvette hissed in a low, spooky voice.

Andie rolled her eyes. Yvette tended to get carried away when it came to conspiracy theories and supernatural beings.

Whenever the fiftysomething artist — er, *artiste*, as she preferred — wasn't bent over her pottery wheel or painting canvases to sell in town, she was investigating paranormal phenomena or communing with spirits. Or so she claimed. Her clothes looked like something out of the Dalai Lama's closet, and her thick blond dreadlocks bounced as she spoke.

"I'm telling you, it's a skinwalker. It's the only explanation."

"Only explanation, my ass," Brady bellowed. "It was probably kids from town, trespassing again. Setting off rumors too, as if I don't have better things to deal with."

Andie peeked at the side of the barn. Despite a recent power-wash, the faint outline of graffiti still showed.

Beware. Skinwalker territory. Enter at your own risk.

Andie hid a grin. The graffiti had been the subject of Brady's previous report, filed on the eve of the first wave of potentials buyers coming to inspect the land. Brady had managed to hide the graffiti with a stack of hay bales before the clients arrived, but not before a local reporter managed to snap a few shots. Ever since then, social media had exploded with tales of a skinwalker rampaging through Yavapai County.

"Damn kids," Brady cursed.

Andie exchanged looks with Arivera. Environmentally minded kids from the local high school had started a petition to save Lazy Q Ranch. But it was a hell of a long way out of town for kids to travel, and it was hard to believe they would go as far as mutilating a cow.

"Whoa, there." The cowboy skittered away as the injured steer swung its horns.

"I swear, it's a skinwalker. I've seen him out at night," Yvette insisted.

Andie sighed quietly. The stories about an evil shaman who could don the fur of a wild beast and wreak havoc in the night were just that — stories. There was bound to be a perfectly rational explanation for anyone willing to look.

Yvette hunched and curved her fingers. "It has to be a skinwalker. Nothing else has claws like that."

The motion mimicked an item from that morning's police briefing, and a connection clicked in Andie's mind.

Claws. Giant chickens, Chavez had joked.

"Actually, there is something else with claws like that," she said. "A cassowary."

If looks could kill, Andie would already be in her grave, and Brady would be on death row.

"Casso-what?" he boomed. "What the hell is that?"

Hansen nodded, latching on to the idea. "You're right."

"How the hell can she be right? And what is she even talking about?"

Andie weighed up whether she could get away with calling Brady an ass. She was off duty, after all. But better not, she supposed.

"A cassowary is a large, flightless Australian bird." She held a hand at eye level to indicate the height. "Like an ostrich, but with really sharp claws. Apparently, they get really aggressive."

Yvette nodded sagely. "Didn't one kill a man in Florida a while back?"

Andie bit back a sigh. That was just the kind of news Yvette would be up on.

"Florida? Australia?" Brady shook his head. "What the hell does that have to do with my ranch?"

Not your ranch, Andie wished she could say.

"A man on the west side of town was illegally keeping exotic animals, and one escaped," she explained. "If it weren't for the neighbors reporting it, we might never have known."

"Fucking typical," Brady muttered. "Do you cops know anything?"

Even calm, collected Hansen went stiff at that. "We know many things, Mr. Brady. Zoning laws, for example. Water rights. Public rights of way..."

It was a barely veiled threat, and Brady knew it. Local police didn't normally have the bandwidth to scrutinize building permits, but if they chose to, who knew what violations they might find?

All that shone through Hansen's unspoken warning. *Just think, Mr. Brady. What might we find if we looked, and how long might that delay progress on your project?*

Arivera shot Andie a grin that said, *My partner is a goddamn genius.*

Actually, Andie had entertained the same idea weeks ago. So far, she'd resisted the temptation to get mixed up in it all.

But only so far, a corner of her mind muttered.

Her eyes drifted to the rocky bluffs, and her thoughts bounced to Buck. If Brady's plans went through, the whole valley would be overrun, and Buck would be driven off — or worse, shot.

As a police officer, she was expected to leave community issues to politicians, so she'd done her best to keep her mouth shut. Speaking out meant risking being transferred to another post — or even worse.

She took in the surroundings one more time. Beyond the ranch perimeter, the desert slumbered, together with all its birds, beasts, insects, and flowers. Was all that worth risking her job for?

Her heart thumped. Yes, it was. For all that, and especially for Buck.

Still, it would be awfully nice if she could figure out a way to prevent runaway development without jeopardizing her job.

"Cassowuddy, huh?" Brady muttered.

"Cassowary," Arivera corrected.

Yvette shook her head. "It's a skinwalker, I tell you."

Andie nearly put her face in her hands. The capacity of some people to cling to implausible explanations never ceased to amaze her.

"Fine." Brady snapped his fingers at a ranch hand. "Rustle up every man and weapon on the ranch. We'll head out at first light and hunt that bird down."

Andie stared. Clearly, the man had seen too many Wild West movies. And, whoa. The last thing Buck needed was a posse of trigger-happy bozos blasting blindly through the underbrush.

"Um..." she started, but Brady cut her off.

"This here is private land. We have every right to defend it from dangerous animals." He turned to Hansen. "Right, Officer?"

Andie bristled. She was an officer too, and Brady knew it.

"Heed my word. It's a skinwalker," Yvette warned. "And it will be back."

Brady scoffed, but the ranch hands looked around, going a little pale.

Yvette turned to the desert and spoke in a spooky voice. "I guarantee, it will be back."

Chapter Five

Roy spent a long time on the ridge, watching the ranch where Andie had gone. Then he sniffed the air and set off to inspect the area for himself. Was something truly wrong, or was it another case of humans making a big fuss about nothing?

Slowly, he crept closer, inspecting every inch of the terrain. But there was no scent of trouble — other than the blustery human kind — and he trotted away again, escaping the glaring lights and noise. Really escaping, driven by that wild side that urged him to stay far from the human world.

Heading for high ground, he loped along a long, undulating ridgeline. Back past Andie's place, then farther and farther. His thoughts slowed down, leaving his mind in a comfortable canine blur. Instinct drove him onward, and nothing really registered other than the earth under his paws and surrounding scents and sounds.

Eventually, he reached a high mesa and stopped, getting his bearings. He was on the very edge of the mesa, overlooking a vast swath of land. A row of dark mountains drew a sawtooth pattern on the northern horizon. To the east was the highway, a ribbon of lights that marked vehicles moving north or south. From this distance, all was silent, the danger remote. Scrubby pastureland spread out below, dotted with the lights of a tiny community.

He took a long, slow breath, considering that place. Twin Moon Ranch.

A place he'd left a long, long time ago. So long ago, he'd almost forgotten why.

Or tried to, anyway.

His tail stuck out stiffly as he peered at the sprawling property. Had that really been home?

Never really home, a bitter part of his mind cursed. *Never really fit in.*

But that was the story of his life, wasn't it? Yearning for some place to fit in.

Moving often as a kid had been hard, as one bad relationship after another kept his mother on the run. Each new place brought fights, insults, and laughter — the mean kind — that cut to the bone. Things started looking up when he'd moved to Twin Moon Ranch, only for fate to strike more cruelly than before.

Roy peered over the cliff's edge, down to the jagged rocks below. It was a lot like the spot where Raymond had fallen to his death, though not quite as high.

An acidic taste filled his mouth. Things would have been so different if he'd been around to keep an eye on his younger brother that night. For Raymond, and for him.

No one had ever understood what exactly had happened, and the strict ranch alpha hadn't shown any interest in investigating. Not for a kid who was always getting into trouble anyway. Human authorities weren't much better, calling it a tragic accident, then closing the book on the case.

I should have been there. I should have kept an eye on him. The familiar refrain haunted him still. Lord knew his mother wasn't up to keeping an eye on either of her sons.

Roy pawed the earth, cutting off the memories there. It didn't matter why he'd drifted away from the ranch. The question was, what was drawing him back now?

Destiny, a deep, distant voice whispered in his mind.

He growled into the night, low and long. Destiny was a force to avoid. In a way, it was like the human world — better to fly under the radar and go unnoticed. That way, neither force could mess around with your life, your heart, or your soul.

And yet, he found himself leaning closer, straining to listen for some call. None came — nothing he could hear, anyway.

But still, he could sense a pull. A little like the pull toward Andie.

But why? Why here? Why now?

He pawed the earth uneasily. Most of the time, destiny's meddling brought trouble. But what if it was finally bringing him something good?

Like Andie, his wolf gushed.

Yes, like Andie. But what was drawing him back to Twin Moon Ranch?

Friends. Community. And most importantly, help when danger appears, a little voice whispered in his mind.

He growled under his breath. Danger… Did that mean whatever was happening at Lazy Q Ranch or something else?

Finally, he turned his back on Twin Moon Ranch and trotted back the way he'd come. To Andie's house.

Yes, there. To a human's home.

If he had any sense, he would run for the mountains instead and never, ever return. Not to Twin Moon Ranch, not to the Lazy Q, not even to Andie. He didn't need any part of the shifter or human world.

But his heart refused to give Andie up, and his feet refused to steer him anywhere but back to her. As he ran, his pulse skipped and his tail wagged. Which was crazy, because Andie was a human, and humans didn't know about loyalty or true love.

And yet, there he went, putting one foot in front of the other as if a magnet were reeling him in. Miles passed, giving him plenty of time to come to his senses and turn around. But he didn't. He couldn't. Instead, he loped all the way back to the boulder by Andie's house. He even covered the last few steps in a sprint, as if something terrible might happen if he weren't there to protect her.

Luckily, the house was peaceful as ever, the lights out for the night. Moonlight bounced off the bumper of Andie's truck, and crickets chirped all around. Closing his eyes, he sniffed and listened long enough to convince himself Andie was inside, breathing the deep, even breaths of sleep.

So, whew. Everything was all right.

Everything but him. Clearly, he didn't have his head screwed on right. What was it about this human that drew him in again and again?

Destiny. The word echoed through his mind.

He froze, finally making the connection. *Mate... Fate... Destiny.*

Only one force could make him feel the way he did about Andie. Destiny. But, hell. You couldn't bow to one of fate's whims without surrendering to many others, so where did that leave him?

His wolf let out a low whine. *I want my mate. Need her.*

He could feel the truth of that deep in his bones, but damn. Where did that leave him?

An owl hooted, making his ear flick.

Who, who, it asked. *Who are you?*

Buck, he wanted to say, because that's who he wanted to be. The soul connected to Andie.

But dark memories chimed in, reminding him who he used to be. Roy.

He gave himself a good shake and lowered his belly to the ground. Enough thinking. It was time to rest.

Good night, Buck, he imagined Andie saying as she'd done so often before.

Good night, a human voice sounded in his mind.

His voice, making him feel closer to his previous life than he had in a long, long time. A life spent mostly in human form, with all its conveniences — like arms to hold his true love. Lips to explain who he was and why he was there. Better yet, lips to kiss her with and let that do the talking for a while.

With a sigh, he dropped his muzzle to the ground. Fantasies were another part of the human world he hadn't missed until now.

Good night, my love.

He imagined saying it from close up, so Andie could hear him... See him... Maybe even touch him — in human form, not as a wolf.

Good night, he imagined her whispering back. *Good night, my mate.*

Chapter Six

Andie stirred in bed, then stretched and looked around. The first rays of sunlight were angling over the eastern hills, wrestling with the chilly winter air. In bed, though, she was snug and warm.

Lying on her right side, facing the big window, made her feel like she was outside. Her left arm stuck out, taking up the empty side of the bed, and for an instant, she imagined a man there.

Just as quickly, she pushed the thought away. Aside from her fellow officers at work, the closest she came to male company these days was a wild wolf.

She sighed and pushed the depressing thought away. Why spoil a perfectly good morning with such somber thoughts?

Instead, she stood and pulled a blanket over her shoulders like a robe. Then she shuffled to the kitchen and mulled over the previous day's events while the kettle boiled.

Big Bird — er, a cassowary — on the run.

Trouble at Lazy Q Ranch.

Buck, her wild wolf friend.

Stirring milk into her coffee, she stepped out into the crisp winter morning. Steam rose from her mug, swirling in the cold desert air.

"Good morning," she whispered over the rim of her mug.

Buck wasn't in sight, which was a damn shame, but there were miles of desert to greet. And if he was out there somewhere, her greeting included him too.

"Watch yourself today," she whispered. "And do your best to come visit tonight."

The morning flew by, but the moment she set off for work in town, time dragged.

She gazed longingly at the hills throughout the day and long after the sun went down. It was a Saturday, which meant she followed up her day job with what Chavez called her side hustle — bartending at the Lone Wolf, a bar on the edge of town.

"It's mostly to help Rita," she insisted when Chavez teased her on the way out of headquarters.

She'd met Rita, the sixtysomething owner of the Lone Wolf, a few years back in responding to a call about a barroom brawl. By the time she and Kyle had raced over to that side of town, Rita had things under control, thanks to a decades-old shotgun and a sharp tongue.

This is just about the only useful thing that no-good husband of mine left when he took off, Rita had muttered, blowing on the shotgun's muzzle like a smoking six-shooter in a classic Western.

So Rita was hardly a pushover. But when Andie learned more about her life... Well, she just had to help. That meant bartending a few times a week, especially weekends — the busiest nights of the week and the most likely to attract the rowdiest clientele.

"Yeah, sure," Chavez had joked. "You work there to help Rita... Or is it to pick up a man?"

She'd gotten so used to his wisecracks, they barely registered any more. But Lee's look did. That look that said, *Seriously, Andie. A great woman like you. When are you going to find yourself a good guy?*

When the world makes one, she probably would have shot back.

It wasn't that she hated all men — or preferred women, as Chavez kept teasing. It was just that the man she dreamed of didn't exist. That, and a decade of police work had slowly taken its toll. There were only so many cases of homicide, rape, or domestic abuse a woman could witness without locking away part of herself.

Anyway, bartending brought in a little extra cash. Maybe even enough to buy her own place someday. That, and she hadn't really had anything better to do on Friday and Saturday nights — or any night, for that matter.

That is, until Buck had come along.

Now, shifts at the Lone Wolf were more of a chore. But the money helped, and it felt good to help Rita out. That didn't stop her from celebrating closing time, though.

"See you, Rita," Andie called once they'd closed down and cleaned up. "See you, Mick." She waved to the bar owner's son.

Minutes later, she was driving away from town and toward home. A lovestruck cowboy crooned over the radio, followed by an ad for used cars. Her mind was already racing ahead, though. Would Buck visit that night?

Her pulse skipped when she pulled into view of the valley, but just as she was coming to her turnoff, a horse raced by, tossing its head. A runaway, with reins hanging loosely. She stomped on the brakes, staring. Wasn't that Chico, Jose's horse?

A moment later, a man ran into view, waving wildly, and she gaped.

"Jose?"

Normally, the goatherd was the picture of calm. Now, he ran up to her truck and banged his hands on the hood.

"Stop. Wait. Help!"

She pushed the door open and stepped out. What was wrong?

Jose grabbed her arm, pointing over the ridge in terror, speaking in a mix of English and Spanish. "Over there... Goats... *Diablo*... At least six..."

She frowned. "Six what?"

"Dead... Ripped apart..."

Nearby bushes swayed as something big moved through them, and Jose whipped around, turning white.

"Skinwalker..."

Andie's pulse had already been climbing. Now, it leaped. Skinwalker?

A moment later, a dog emerged from the bush, and she exhaled. "It's just Lucky. Come on, boy."

Whimpering, the big dog took two steps forward, then one step back. He was shaking, though uninjured, as Andie ascertained once she finally coaxed the dog over.

"Good dog, Lucky. Good dog. Are you okay?"

He seemed fine, though just as shaken as Jose. The goatherd couldn't get out more than a word or two at a time as she led him around to the passenger side and helped him in. Then she dropped the tailgate and did her best to coax Lucky up. In the end, it took lifting his front paws to the edge and a hard shove from behind to get the big dog in. Then she flipped the tailgate closed and slid back into the driver's seat, trying to decide what to do. Should she track Jose's horse or his herd? Get help? Call in an incident to headquarters, even?

She looked at her phone on the dashboard, mulling that option over. But Jose shook his head.

"No police. Please."

It took her a moment to understand why. Lots of farmhands were undocumented and thus avoided the police. It was nice to know Jose trusted her, but damn. That didn't leave her too many options for outside help.

"Tell me again," she tried. "What happened?"

Getting the story out of Jose was harder than getting a 140-pound dog into her truck, but she did, one shaky word at a time. A few of Jose's goats had wandered away, and he'd searched for them for half the night. When he finally found them...

"Skinwalker," he whispered as if one might be waiting to pounce from the back seat.

He went on in such detail that she almost started to believe him. But Jose, like a lot of other folks in this part of the West, believed in all kinds of spirits, curses, and ghosts.

"That way." He pointed a shaky finger.

She drove, following a barely there track that kept her vehicle's speed to a crawl.

"Down there." He indicated a hollow to the left.

Andie pulled over and looked. But the headlights threw as many shadows as they illuminated, and she couldn't see a thing.

"Wait." Jose grabbed her arm when she pushed the door open. "Don't go out. It could still be out there."

Andie pursed her lips. Now wasn't the time to explain that skinwalkers didn't exist.

"At least take a gun." Jose gestured to the glove compartment, assuming she carried one.

Well, she didn't. Statistics showed that nearly one in five police officers killed were shot with their own or a partner's weapon, and sadly, her dad had been one of them. So, no. Andie had no interest in compounding that statistic by toting a gun in her off-duty time.

"It'll be fine," she assured him, heading out into the darkness with a utility-grade flashlight in her hand. Ninety-nine percent of the dangers in life stemmed from people, and there was no one around.

She made her way forward slowly, swinging the flashlight, lighting up a prickly pear. . . a bushy acacia. . . animal tracks. . .

Back in the pickup, Lucky whined, and Jose whispered hoarsely. "Andie. . ."

She shone the light on the animal tracks. Lots and lots of clove-hoofed tracks. The goats had been through here, all right.

Step by step, she followed the tracks into the hollow. Then she jumped onto a rock and shone the light in slow, steady arcs.

No goats. No movement. Nothing but the desert. But then something caught her eye, and she backed up the beam of light. A split second later, she stopped abruptly, staring at a leg.

A single leg. And not far away, the rest of the carcass.

Flashlights weren't too good at bringing out color at night, but the dark splotches on the ground could only be blood. Lots of it.

One pool connected to another as she swung the light around. Another carcass. More blood. Yet another lifeless lump. And another, and another, strewn about as if a grenade had gone off.

A decade of law enforcement had exposed her to lots of grisly sights, but even so, her stomach lurched. She inched forward, studying the wounds on the nearest goat.

Yikes. Those were long, ugly slashes, not gunshots or bites. Jose wasn't kidding when he'd said *ripped apart.*

Still, there were a lot of possible explanations, like that giant bird that she'd been searching for over the past few days. Cassowaries were known for their razor-sharp claws, right?

Then again, how likely was it for a single bird to kill so many goats?

All right, then, a band of coyotes. That was more likely. Possibly feral dogs...mountain lions...or even a wolf.

Her breath caught there. Buck?

She gulped, studying the nearest goat. Buck couldn't be responsible for such a cruel act, could he? Hunting for food was fine, but killing for the thrill of it?

Her heart sank as she looked around, and she sent out a little prayer.

Please, no. Not Buck.

A bush swayed, and a chill went down her back. Standing dead still, she shone her light into the darkness.

"Andie..." Jose called, sounding more nervous than ever.

She frowned. Damn the man for giving her spooky vibes.

But, shit. That bush over there was swaying, and another one nearby, as if something had snuck along, out of sight.

Slowly, she backed up. Maybe she ought to wait for daylight to inspect this isolated, blood-drenched place.

It was a skinwalker, I tell you, Jose had said. *I saw its eyes. A pair of red eyes, staring through the night.*

Andie jerked her head up as another bush swayed.

When Chico galloped off, I thought I was done for...

She swung the light around. Still nothing. But that was scary too. Not a bird peeped, not an insect chirped.

The moon slid behind a cloud. Back in the truck, Lucky whined. An acacia scratched Andie's leg as she backed through the brush. She glanced over her shoulder. How far was her pickup now?

Then a twig snapped, and her blood ran cold.

Something was stalking her. Creeping closer...closer...

Andie kept up her measured steps, ordering herself not to turn tail and flee. Telling herself that flash of red was her imagination, not a pair of murderous eyes. Telling herself everything was okay, even though something deep in her soul said, *Far from.*

"Andie!" Jose hissed.

A growl sounded from the bush. It wasn't Lucky, whose nails clicked as he paced in the back of the pickup. It wasn't the beast stalking her either. The growl was long and low, coming from the right.

She peered into the darkness, more nervous than ever. But then she made out the outline of a wolf, and her hopes soared. Buck?

The tension in the air spiked as if every desert dweller knew trouble was coming and they had to take cover. Too bad she wasn't a jackrabbit that could sprint to safety or a gopher that could burrow away.

On the other side of the hollow, claws scraped over the dry earth, and a pair of red points flashed.

Run, a voice sounded in her mind. *Go, quick.*

That had to be instinct kicking in, but for some reason, she pictured Buck calling to her. Which was as crazy as the idea of a skinwalker was.

No such thing as skinwalkers, she told herself.

The glowing red points shone brighter, mocking her. *You sure about that?*

"Andie!" Jose called, hoarse and quiet, like a kid reporting a monster under the bed.

Grrr, Buck growled a bitter warning to his foe.

Just then, Andie bumped into her pickup and spun around.

"Get in! Go! Go!" Jose whisper-yelled.

Andie jumped in, started the engine, and threw the pickup into reverse. Bushes groaned and wheels spun as she tore through a tight turn, then took off ten times faster than she had come in.

Her eyes jumped to the rearview window, not sure what to expect. Skinwalker? Wolf? Neither?

Before she caught a clear look, the pickup crossed the ridge, and the view was concealed. Good thing? Bad thing?

Andie didn't know. But one thing was for sure. She hadn't been the only living beast in the hollow that night.

Chapter Seven

Roy bared his teeth and growled into the darkness. What the hell had that been? He'd only gotten a glimpse of two glowing eyes and whiff of a weird, bitter smell before the creature in the hollow ran off.

He'd been sorely tempted to give chase, but it was more important to see Andie home safely. By the time he had, it was too late to go after that monster, whatever it had been.

Instead, he stood on a rise near Andie's house, panting and wondering what to do. She'd dropped the goatherd and dog off at the ranch, then sped home at twice her usual speed. Once there, she'd hurried inside and locked all the doors and windows. That made sense, but part of him still mourned. She wasn't afraid of him, was she?

He paced, still baring his teeth. He'd been patiently awaiting Andie all evening, and the wind was from the north, so he hadn't noticed any foul play until it was too late. He'd only happened across the gruesome scene in the hollow a short time before Andie had arrived, and he'd only stayed long enough to start tracking whatever had mauled the poor beasts. Unfortunately, Jose had come along with his dog about that time, so Roy had given up and hightailed over to Andie's place, more intent than ever on keeping her safe. But then panic-stricken Jose had intercepted Andie and led her directly to the crime scene.

He gnashed his teeth. That man was a fool. What if Andie had been hurt?

And, shit. Now his own wolf tracks were all over the hollow. What if those dead goats were blamed on him?

He went back to growling under his breath. Something was afoot. Something evil. He wasn't sure what it was after, but he knew it was no good.

Then an ugly thought struck him, and he froze. All those wolf tracks...

He gritted his teeth, scouring his memories. All those times he'd blanked out, finding himself miles from where he'd last been...

What if the warnings were true? The ones that urged shifters not to stay in animal form for too long at the risk of losing your mind. Was that happening to him?

He pictured the carnage, then shook his head. There was no way he'd done that. No way. He'd spotted the perpetrator, and Andie had too.

He took a couple of deep breaths, swearing to himself it hadn't been him. After another long, mournful minute of studying Andie's house, he retreated into the darkness to think. As much as he burned to stay and protect Andie, her movements were too unpredictable for him to follow in wolf form.

That left the option of hunting down the mystery beast on his own, which had a hell of a lot of appeal to his impulsive, animal side.

He charged off into the desert night, intent on doing exactly that. But as skilled a tracker as he was, it was hard. The beast had barely left a scent in the air and only strangely scattered tracks on the ground. The few faint traces Roy found confused the hell out of him. The tracks only went so far before disappearing into thin air, then reappeared a dozen yards away, as if the creature were capable of huge, hopping leaps. He couldn't pin down the scent, either — a weird mix of canine muskiness and the thick, downier scent of bird. Which was it, dammit?

Then there was the carnage the beast had inflicted — and worst of all, the cold, prickly sensation it had left in its wake. It was spooky as hell, as if an evil spirit had crept over the landscape rather than an ordinary beast.

Roy stood still, testing the wind. Then he set off to the east. Farther and farther, then up a long, rough trail. Finally, he reached the top of the big mesa and trotted to the far side. There, he sat, considering.

Twin Moon Ranch, home to the strongest wolf pack in the Desert Southwest. Would they be of any help?

Every muscle in his body tensed at the idea. He'd left the ranch years ago, vowing never to return. Was he really willing to go there now?

Well, yes, because he would do anything for Andie.

Still, not everyone at Twin Moon was reliable, nor was everyone a friend. Asking them for help would be a gamble — for him, as well as for Andie.

Surely there was a better way. But what?

He tapped his tail slowly, considering. As a wolf, he could never be part of Andie's world. He would never be more than a canine companion.

He closed his eyes at the ache for more. Much more.

As a man, we can be more, his human side insisted. *We can touch her. Hold her. Kiss her. And so much more...*

Heat shot through his core, and intense yearning swept over his soul. He wanted her. Needed her. Most importantly, she needed him. Not just the wolf, but the man. He could sense it deep in his soul.

Correction, a little voice told him. *She needs both: the wolf and the man.*

It made sense. As a wolf, he could protect her from whatever evil lurked out there. As a man, he could fill the gap in her soul — a gap that echoed his own. Only together could they be whole.

Destiny... the whisper sounded again, making him shiver.

But there was no denying the truth. Andie was his destined mate. She had to be.

She will be, his wolf insisted.

And just like that, a switch flipped in him. A guy could hide from fate, or he could head out like a knight riding boldly to take on a dragon. He could make his own fate, dammit.

He stood straighter. His mate needed him, and he would do anything necessary to help her. Even leaving the comfortable limbo he'd occupied in the wild.

So, yes. He had to assume human form — but he didn't need the wolves of Twin Moon Ranch for that.

Looking down at his paws, he tried to remember what hands felt like. He wiggled the digits, imagining them growing thinner, longer, and without tufts of fur.

Second thoughts set in, and he gritted his teeth. Maybe he was better off sticking to canine form.

But a renegade part of his mind insisted, reminding him of all the things a human body was good for, such as being close to his mate.

So he closed his eyes again, focusing on the only thing that gave shifting any allure.

Andie.

He pictured cupping her cheek. Holding her hand. Smiling at her without flashing long, pointy incisors, and seeing her smile back.

Arms would also come in handy. He could wrap them around her and hold her close. Lips too, because they would allow him to speak in a way Andie would understand.

Lips would let us kiss too, his wolf hummed.

Yes, a human body would let him fulfill every desire mates shared.

His thoughts glided away on heated fantasies for a while. Then he dipped his head, lowered his tail, and made the transition to human form. A painfully long, clunky process that made him moan. Damn, was he out of practice. An eternity later, he blinked and looked down.

Two feet, not four. Two hands. Ten fingers. No tail.

No fur either, exposing him to winter's chill. Clearer eyesight was a plus, but that was a poor trade-off for a dull sense of smell. He squinted against the color seeping into his vision, nearly as overwhelming as bright lights could be. Still, he'd done it. He was in human form!

He swayed, trying to order his feet into action. But that was hard, with only two stilt-like legs to balance on instead of four. That and a glance over his body made him stop and scowl.

As a wolf, everything had seemed so simple. Now, details reared their ugly heads — like the fact that he couldn't just burst into Andie's home naked in the middle of the night. That much, even he knew.

He looked around, reassessing his plan. Clothes. He needed clothes. But where?

Briefly, he considered the homestead of Lazy Q Ranch. But the bright lights put him off, as did the prospect of barking dogs. What he needed was a place where no one was home.

He turned east, toward the little house way out on the other edge of the ranch. Bingo. He'd been through the area often enough to know a single woman lived there and that a man used to stay in the trailer nearby. It was late enough that the lights in both places were off, and he hadn't seen the man for weeks, which meant the trailer was unoccupied.

Perfect, his wolf growled.

So perfect, he forgot he was in human form, and his first shaky step brought a bare foot down on a thorn. For the next few seconds, he bounced around on one foot, suppressing a howl.

Human feet, his wolf muttered. *Useless.*

Roy sighed, gingerly placed his bare foot back down, and shifted back to wolf form.

Much better. His wolf practically pranced along.

Minutes later, he was edging around the corner of the property, then stealing up to the trailer. His second shift to human form wasn't quite as awkward as the first, thank goodness. The trailer door wasn't locked, but it did squeak. Easing it open was torture, but then he was inside. And, jackpot — an entire dresser full of clothes stood open to him. He rifled through it, then tried on a pair of pants. They were too big, so he tried several more. The trailer was tiny, though, and he knocked a lamp over with a crash.

He froze, listening for a long time. Then he eased back into motion and resumed his search. Alarms clanged in his mind, because it was taking too long. But how long was it, actually? Time passed differently in human form — sometimes agonizingly slowly, other times much too fast. So much so, he couldn't keep track.

He gave his head a shake. Either way, he had to find some clothes soon.

An eternity later, he cursed and went back to a pair of jeans he'd discarded earlier. They would have to do — if he found a belt to cinch them tight. That took forever, but he eventually found one and went about feeding the damn thing through the belt loops on the jeans — a challenging task for fumbling fingers more used to paw form. Finally, he succeeded and started pulling on the jeans. Right leg in the one side, left leg in the other...

He'd just worked the jeans three-quarters of the way up his naked body when the door burst open along with a blinding light.

"Freeze! Hands up!" someone yelled.

Every muscle in his body tensed, and his inner wolf bared its teeth.

"Don't move!" the intruder shouted.

He was about to bowl them aside and sprint out the door, when he stopped cold. Wait. He knew that voice, although he'd never heard it in that cold, commanding tone.

Andie! Andie! His wolf wagged its tail.

But his human side sank as he threw a hand up and squinted into the light. He'd dreamed of standing eye-to-eye with Andie so many times. But not like this.

Definitely not like this.

Chapter Eight

Andie blinked and tightened her grip around her Smith & Wesson 13. If there was such a thing as a standard arrest, this was definitely not it.

For one thing, Yvette was half a step behind her, wrapped in a fluffy pink robe and hefting a shotgun.

For another, the perpetrator was naked from the knees up. His sideways stance hid his private parts, but only just.

Still, an arrest was an arrest, no matter how far up — or down — the perpetrator's pants might be, or how perfectly sculpted his abs were.

"Don't move," she repeated, mostly to focus on the task at hand.

"Right," Yvette breathed, soaking in the sight. "Stay right there."

Andie braced herself, because every perpetrator she'd ever apprehended reacted in one of two ways — either he would make a break for it or start pleading his case.

But this guy just stood there, staring at her.

And, yikes. She couldn't help but stare back at those warm brown eyes. They were honest. . . innocent. . . strong, but a little wounded, too.

Her police mind catalogued all that in the space of a heartbeat, and sympathy swirled in the cauldron of emotions she kept in a separate compartment of her soul. That was the way it was — after so many years on the force, you just knew. This man wasn't a danger to society, just down on his luck in one of a thousand tragic ways she'd borne witness to over the years.

That kind of man, she'd come across before. But this one was strikingly familiar in a way she couldn't explain. That square jaw and that wiry, outdoorsman build. The wavy brown hair that begged her to step closer and finger-comb it back behind his ears. Those fathoms-deep eyes that hid as much as they revealed.

Her mind turned the details over again and again, trying to find a match. Had they gone to kindergarten together? Maybe someone from the Lone Wolf bar? Or was he a former pro cowboy who seemed familiar because he'd featured in some ads before his luck turned and he'd ended up on the skids?

Whatever it was, she could have sworn she knew him.

Still, she kept her weapon up. Her father had misjudged an arrest once, and it had cost him his life.

"Pants up, then hands on your head." She jerked her weapon up slightly.

Still, he just stood there — so long, she wondered if he was deaf. But then he pulled the jeans over his hips and slowly raised his hands to his head. The motion made every muscle in his torso ripple, eliciting a muffed sigh from Yvette.

"This is private property. Is that clear to you?" Andie said, trying to get a gauge on him.

His nostrils flared a little, but he didn't reply.

"Breaking and entering is a crime, sir. Can you explain why you're here?"

That much seemed obvious from the clothes tossed on the bed and around the floor, but his gaze didn't dart there. He kept his eyes firmly on hers, and when his lips parted, she felt sure he would say, *For you. I'm here because of you.*

But he didn't utter a word, and Andie discarded the notion immediately. Why was her imagination on overdrive?

Besides, none of it made sense. What man would break in to a trailer to steal ill-fitting clothes? Where were the clothes he'd come in? How had he gotten there? There was no sign of a vehicle, and no one could have hitchhiked so far off the main road.

She pulled her badge out with her free hand. "Police. Last chance to explain before I call in a squad car."

Yikes. Wait a minute. Why was she giving him the benefit of the doubt?

His lips twitched, but no sound came out. It was strange, how totally switched on his senses seemed. But when it came to human interactions, he was definitely on the slow side.

Yvette touched her arm in a gesture that said, *Give him a moment.*

Andie nearly rolled her eyes. When Yvette had rung for help twenty minutes earlier, her voice had been hushed and urgent.

Andie! I need you to come over right now!

Andie had squinted sleepily at the clock as Yvette rushed on. *At first, I thought it was the skinwalker, but I think it's just a man.*

Definitely a man, Andie thought, trying not to ogle his athletic frame.

He's in the trailer right now, probably robbing me blind. Then Yvette had dropped her voice and whispered, *He could be a rapist, you know.*

Then he would be in your bedroom, Andie had nearly snorted, but she had driven over right away. And here she was now, in the midst of one of the strangest arrests she'd ever made.

An arrest Yvette was definitely not helping with. She'd gone from frantic on the phone to outright combative, hefting that rusty shotgun. But now that Yvette had decided the intruder was harmless — and strikingly handsome — she suddenly went all coy.

"Maybe I should get us some coffee," Yvette cooed.

"No coffee," Andie barked. "And you..." She wiggled her gun at the trespasser. "Sit."

Oops. That came out more harshly than she'd meant it to. And boy, did the man look hurt.

"I need you to sit, sir," she said more gently. "Standard procedure. Right there on the floor. Keep your hands on your head."

She spoke in the softer tone she used on sensitive cases to convey *I know things are a mess right now, but if we both keep our cool, everything will be all right. We'll figure this all out, and we'll get you the help you need to straighten out.*

And hey, sometimes it really did work out that way. Whenever a case touched her heart — and too many did — she made sure to follow up, doing her best to get folks into suitable rehabilitation programs or steady jobs, together with the help of her contacts in social services.

It was like her dad used to say. *It's not my job to put people in jail. It's to help everyone in the community live a good, clean life.*

That attitude had earned her dad Officer of the Year three times in a distinguished twenty-year career back in LA.

Then again, it had also gotten him killed.

Without taking her eyes off the intruder, Andie pulled out her phone and handed it to Yvette. "Dial six, please. I need to contact headquarters."

But Yvette hesitated, and for some reason, Andie did too. The whole world seemed to slow down around her, until time went still. Everything faded away, leaving her attention trained entirely on the man.

Do I know you from somewhere? she nearly whispered.

His eyes seemed to glow. *Yes, you do. The same way I know you.*

Not that ether of them uttered a word. They just stood there, dumb struck as a deep, earthy voice echoed through Andie's mind.

Destiny.

The way his eyes glowed made her wonder if he'd heard it too. Soulful, trusting eyes. Eyes that pleaded with her to understand some secret he kept carefully locked away.

Time ticked by silently, but somehow, she couldn't move. Outside, grass rustled and crickets chirped. A roadrunner scampered past, and the scent of sage wafted in the air. The serene nighttime scene she loved so much was playing out as it always did, and it was impossible not to picture sitting out on her rock, studying the stars. She even pictured Buck, watching her as she took it all in.

Then she blinked, pulling herself together — and, yikes. This man was gazing at her in exactly the same way. Not threatening, not intruding. Just taking her in like another wondrous thing.

She banged a hand against her own thigh. Man oh man, it was a good thing she didn't work the night shift. Her brain didn't function properly at this late hour. So what if this man was sitting before her, bare-chested and beautiful, even in those ill-fitting jeans? No reason to lose focus, right?

She elbowed Yvette, indicating the phone. "Dial six and put it on speaker, please. I need to call this in to headquarters."

Yvette hesitated, looking at the phone, then the man. "Are you sure that's necessary?"

Andie shot her a disbelieving look that said, *You were the one who called in a panic.*

That was before I found out how innocent he seems. Yvette's eyelids fluttered a little. *Not to mention how handsome.*

Andie formed a thin line with her lips, but Yvette leaned in to whisper.

"Seriously. What if I didn't want to press charges?"

Andie kept her eyes firmly on the intruder, wondering what her father would do. Wondering if it was a case like this he'd fatally misjudged.

"Yvette..." she warned in a whisper-hiss. "He could have a record. He could be on a most-wanted list."

Yvette snorted. "Most wanted to pose for a calendar, maybe." Before Andie could dismiss that, Yvette plowed on. "Seriously. You can tell as well as I that this is not a man who belongs in jail."

"That's for a judge to decide," Andie replied.

The thing was, Yvette's arguments echoed the ones running through her mind.

"Come on," Yvette pleaded. "You can't arrest him. He's no criminal."

Andie knew she damned well could, but still. She couldn't quite start reading this man his Miranda rights. Not with a clear conscience.

You have the right to remain silent...

That part would be a no-brainer for this guy, who was still sitting wordlessly like a dog in an animal shelter: eyes wary yet hopeful, giving her that *Please give me a chance* look.

Still, she had to stand firm. Didn't she?

Anything you say can and will be used against you in a court of law...

She winced, picturing a judge slamming a gavel. Best case, this guy might get off with a fine and community service. Worst case, he'd be locked up. And, shit. Jail had a way of making decent men into criminals even if they'd started with one dumb mistake instead of a hard crime.

You have the right to an attorney. If you cannot afford an attorney, one will be provided for you...

That would be the next part, and he sure looked like he couldn't afford it.

"Seriously. If I don't press charges, you can't arrest him, right?" Yvette tried.

Andie nearly said, *A police officer can arrest anyone with due cause.*

But in this case... Damn. What should she do?

"Come on, Andie," Yvette pleaded.

Andie tuned her out, studying the man instead. Making the wrong call could mean destroying an innocent man's life — or letting a dangerous criminal loose.

Her heart thumped, low and heavy, and memories of her father rushed through her mind. God, what should she do?

Chapter Nine

Roy leaned on the shovel, tipped back his hat, and stared at the startlingly blue desert sky. It was strange, the twists life took. Because it was the next day, and he was in human form, working for Lazy Q Ranch instead of languishing in jail.

The previous night still had his mind spinning. First, the surprise of Andie aiming a gun at him. Then the mind-numbing joy of having her so close. He'd nearly reached out to brush her cheek, just as he'd done in his dreams. For a moment, he was ready to surrender totally to destiny. Because even his imagination hadn't prepared him for the electric feeling of standing eye-to-eye with his mate. Stunning green-brown eyes, exactly the color he'd pictured for so long.

His cheeks had heated, and a low hum sounded in his ears — the sound of blood rushing, synapses firing, or simply the sound of joy welling up like springwater over parched terrain.

Mate, he'd nearly hummed. But he hadn't been able to speak. Hell, he couldn't even move.

Andie had been in pretty much the same state, though he sensed her shaking it off to talk to Yvette. Their words had drifted past him the way human speech drifted past wolf ears — so many disjointed syllables not adding up to anything clear. If he'd strained to tune in, he would have understood, but he didn't have the brain capacity at the time. All he could do was relish that moment with his mate.

In human form and on two feet, he was an inch or two taller than Andie. In wolf form, he had to crane his neck to see her face. Now, he could study every feature, from the graceful curves of her eyebrows all the way to the sharp line of her chin.

Not that he got much farther, because his gaze bounced back to her lips and stayed there.

So close. So perfectly matched to his.

Come on, Yvette had pleaded with Andie. *Give him a break. No harm done, right?*

Roy had barely registered the words. He'd been too busy imagining touching those lips and touching Andie's long, silky hair.

Some people just get down on their luck, Yvette had told Andie next.

That was funny, because he felt like the luckiest guy in the world. He was a man, and Andie was a woman. Same species — well, close enough, if you ignored his shifter side.

So, heck. Maybe he shouldn't have waited so long to shift back to human form.

On the other hand, being human had its issues, which had gradually dawned on him. Things Andie told Yvette, like *trespassing* and *breaking and entering.*

He closed his eyes. Oops. Maybe he should have thought things through a little more.

He hadn't said much, praying that Andie felt what he did. That they were meant to be together, even if they weren't there yet. Destiny was at work, for better or worse, and he would do his damnedest to make sure things went their way.

What are you doing here anyway? Andie had demanded at some point. *Where did you come from?*

It had taken a while for him to croak out a couple of words. He was that out of practice and that overwhelmed.

I lived out there, he'd finally managed, pointing to the hills. *Been away for a long, long time.*

That was just the bare bones of it, but both women softened. Maybe they understood, given how they both lived way out in the back of beyond. Were they, too, tempted to turn their backs on the human world? Was this as far as a non-shifter could go?

Yvette got to brewing the coffee, jabbering the whole time. *I know what it feels like, kid. The world is a mess, and some-*

times, it's easier just to hide away. But you've got to man up and face the music too, right?

He'd only answered in a nod, but it must have communicated more, because Andie had finally relented, letting Yvette have her way.

So, no arrest. No jail. Just Yvette fussing over him like an old auntie slicking up a kid for confirmation day. By dawn, he had an armful of clothes, a pair of boots, and even a bolo tie — for what, he had no clue. Yvette had shoved all that into a pair of old saddlebags, then sat him down and gone at his hair with scissors and a comb — all under the watchful eye of Andie, who kept her gun drawn the whole time.

Don't you worry, dearie, Yvette had promised. *We'll get you back on your feet.*

Which she had — literally — marching him off to the neighboring ranch at first light.

"Brady!" Yvette hollered after ten hard thumps on the door.

"Um, Yvette..." Andie warned, not sounding too convinced.

Neither was Roy. Wasn't Brady the jerk who'd given Andie a hard time not too far back?

It was, and he was just as blustery at six a.m. as he'd been that evening not too long ago.

"What the hell do you want?" Brady barked when he finally stumbled to the door.

"I hear you ran off a couple more ranch hands," Yvette snipped.

Brady had just scowled and kicked the dirt. "Superstitious fools." Spittle flew from his lips, and every drop carried the scent of stale beer. "I kept telling them there's no such thing as a skinwalker, but they still up and left."

Yvette humphed and smacked Roy on the back. "Well, I got you a new hand." Then she folded her arms smugly. "You're welcome."

Brady scowled, though he did turn a horse trader's eye to Roy.

"You believe in ghosts and crazy legends, kid?"

Roy thought it over. If shifters counted as crazy legends. . .
Well, yes. Not that he uttered a word.

"You ready to work hard?" Brady went on hollering like a
sergeant breaking in a new recruit.

The idea of working for Brady had zero appeal, but otherwise, the job suited his means. Andie's place was just a stone's
throw away, which meant he could keep an eye on her — and
any encroaching danger — in human or in wolf form. He could
work on gaining her trust and someday, somehow, make her
his mate.

So he'd nodded in agreement, and that was that. He didn't
catch — or care — what the job paid, but he knew it came
with a bed in an eerily empty bunkhouse and meals cooked by
Jose.

"As long as he doesn't go and quit too," Brady had muttered under his breath.

Roy blinked a few times and glanced at Andie. Quit? No,
sir. He wouldn't be quitting anytime soon.

But, whew. What a night.

∞∞∞

A week passed, and each day, he grew more accustomed to
being human. Some of it was nice, enjoying the view from six
feet up or scratching an itch with his hands instead of a foot.
That, and nimbly manipulating whatever he wanted with all
those fingers and two incredibly useful thumbs.

Of course, he still turned in bed three times before settling
down to sleep, and he missed the efficiency of his long, wolf
tongue. But it wasn't like he could never shift back. He was
just relearning human ways, one day at a time.

Learning a new job was part of it too. Or relearning,
maybe, because work at the Lazy Q was a lot like the work
he'd done on Twin Moon Ranch. Digging an irrigation trench
here, repairing a fence there, feeding and watering the last few
head of steer. On the whole, the work was superficial — not
so much aimed at keeping the ranch running as to keep up
appearances for potential buyers of subplots of land.

"City folk want to see what they want to see," Brady had grumbled. "Grazing cows. Jingling bells. Goats, too, and lambs. God, they're suckers for lambs. But they want it all far enough away that they don't get bothered by flies when they're lounging by their pools."

Not that any potential buyers visited, not now that word of trouble had spread. A handful of sensation-seekers made their way down the long, lonely road, but either Brady chased them off or Yvette invited them over to the makeshift art gallery she'd set up on her porch. Roy wasn't sure which was worse.

"Ain't it something?" Yvette had prompted when he'd gone over to help one afternoon.

She'd stuck raven feathers onto a sheet of corrugated iron and airbrushed in a weird, twisted figure which lent the artwork its name: *Flight of the Skinwalker*.

But heck, he had Yvette to thank for his turn of luck, so he'd kept his reply neutral.

"It sure is," he murmured, devoting the next hour to helping her set up her little gallery.

For the most part, time passed the same way it had when he'd been in wolf form. Hours just ghosted by, making it hard to say afterward what exactly he'd done, where, or even why.

But when it came to any interaction with Andie — even the briefest moments, and even from afar — time stood still, and the magic of the moment etched itself into his mind for eternity.

He memorized it all. The way her eyes scanned the ranch, then lit up on seeing him. The way her mustang-brown hair swayed in the wind, like a real-life pony's tail. The pattern of freckles on her sun-bronzed cheeks, and the smooth lines of her long, filly legs.

She would make a good wolf, his animal side sighed.

His chest rose and fell in a sigh. *She sure would.*

He'd had plenty of opportunity to observe her over the week, because Andie kept as close an eye on him as he did on her. Sometimes from a distance and sometimes from closer up.

At first, she'd merely rolled her pickup to a crawl on her way to or from work to exchange a few words with him. Things like, *How's the job?* or *Everything okay?* or whatever else cops said to folks they kept an eye on.

"Doing just fine, thanks," he would reply, with the words forming more smoothly day by day.

After two or three days, Andie had warmed up a little and offered a few more words. Things like *That fence looks like it's coming along,* or *I see you're on to the irrigation trench today. Jack-of-all-trades, huh?*

It was funny, because years ago, he'd hated the chitchat humans wasted so much time on. Now, he understood. It was more about connection than the words themselves.

And boy, did he savor that connection, no matter how tenuous it was.

Those were his interactions with Andie the officer, who kept up a cautious, professional front. Even better was Andie the stargazer, whom he visited at night, creeping out of the bunkhouse to shift into wolf form.

"Buck! You're back! You're okay!" The relief in her voice that first night made his heart swell.

He'd nearly run over and rubbed his furry side against her leg but settled for wagging his tail from a distance instead.

Of course I'm here. I will always come to you, my mate, he willed her to understand.

"You been doing good?" she asked.

His tail wagged harder. *Yes, because I get to be close to you more often now.*

"What a week," Andie sighed.

He licked his lips. It sure had been.

So, in some ways, some things hadn't changed, while others had. Andie had started locking her windows and doors at night, making part of him mourn. Still, he couldn't blame her for being cautious — not with the specter of an unknown enemy on the prowl.

That, and a whole lot more to fret about too.

Wolf tracks — *his* tracks — had been spotted at the scene of the goat massacre. That made him a suspect, even though he'd only come across the scene of the crime after the dirty deed was done.

Meanwhile, the true perpetrator was still at large. Namely, the skinwalker — or prankster, depending whether you believed Yvette or Brady. Either way, it posed a threat for all shifters when humans got all abuzz with rumors of supernatural beings. Human curiosity and fear had set off crazed witchhunts centuries ago, driving some shifters to the brink of extinction, while pushing others into hiding or into new territory — including way out here in the American Southwest. All that had been long enough ago to be treated as exaggerated legends these days, but there was no telling what trouble rumors could stir up, even in a modern day and age.

In short, the skinwalker matter had to be solved within the shifter world and as soon as possible. Roy was obliged to do his part — including an abiding duty to his pack at Twin Moon Ranch.

He paused there. Did he mean his pack or his former pack?

Then he shook his head. Technicalities didn't matter. What did matter was putting an end to the skinwalker issue once and for all.

The thing was, whatever it was that had been causing trouble in the area had quieted down. Maybe even gone away, as Brady proposed.

"Gone for good, I hope," the ranch manager had grumbled, wrapping up one of his daily tirades.

Roy sniffed the breeze. Probably more like the calm before the storm. But only time would tell. And if — when? — the beast returned, one thing was for sure. Roy would be there, ready to guard his mate's life.

Chapter Ten

"Everything okay, honey?" Rita, the owner of the Lone Wolf, asked.

Andie gave herself a shake and went back to pouring a draft. "Just overthinking things, I guess." She forced a tight smile.

"As usual." Rita gave her a motherly tap on the arm. "As a smart woman once told me, you gotta take things one step at a time."

Andie faked a grin at the echo of her own words. For a change, her thoughts weren't occupied with solving big social issues. Just a handsome, mysterious, six-foot-one issue.

Namely, Roy, her sort-of-criminal/sort-of-hot new neighbor. Okay, really hot, what with those dark, innocent eyes, quiet voice, and ten-out-of-ten build.

The thing was, guys she'd arrested — or nearly arrested — weren't supposed to occupy her mind for days, and they certainly weren't supposed to inspire steamy, sheet-tossing dreams — especially not in a woman who hadn't been turned on in years. And that, she blamed on her job, dammit. Years of police work had exposed her to the worst in mankind, and being a female officer meant she was called in on nearly every case of rape or domestic abuse. As a consequence, it had become impossible to imagine the physical act of sex as pleasurable in any way, and her libido had shut down.

But all of a sudden, it was back with a vengeance, filling her nights with fantasies of getting it on with Cowboy Scrumptious, as Yvette called Roy.

"Here you go — two drafts," she murmured, summoning just enough focus to deliver them to a couple of truckers seated at the bar.

They flashed smiles and went back to what had become everyone's favorite topic — skinwalkers and the recent troubles at Lazy Q Ranch.

Andie gritted her teeth, holding back a muttered, *No such thing as skinwalkers, guys. Can't you talk football for a change?*

"I need a burger and an order of nachos," Carla, the waitress, called into the kitchen, then glanced around. "Not too busy tonight — so far. Let's hope it stays this way."

A group of regulars clustered around the pool table, while a trio of mellow cowboys played cards at the nearest table. Rita was checking on her son, Mick, who occupied his usual place over on one side, watching the football game on the big-screen TV. Two older couples took the table beside Mick, laughing over old times.

Andie took a deep breath, trying to limit her thoughts to that particular place and time. Mindfulness, they called it, or so she'd heard. The problem was, her thoughts were like so many mustangs — just when she had them mustered, they would whinny and gallop for all four points of the compass.

But, heck. Maybe thoughts could conjure the real thing, because at that very moment, Yvette walked through the door with Cowboy Scrumptious — er, Roy — in tow.

"Yoo-hoo! Andie!" Yvette waved cheerily.

She steered Roy over to the bar — literally, the way one might steer a wheelbarrow or a stubborn mule — and sat him down on the last barstool. Then she hustled over to Andie and leaned in, though Andie spoke first.

"What are you doing, bringing him here?" she whisper-hissed.

Yvette winked. "Making your day, honey. I've seen how you look at Roy."

Andie's cheeks heated. "I do not look at him."

Yvette snorted. "Nothing to be ashamed of, honey. Not when a man looks like that." Her grin stretched, and her eyes warmed. "Besides, I was right. He's a real sweetheart. He's been over to help me every evening, you know."

Andie nodded wearily. Yvette had been stopping by regularly to report on Cowboy Scrumptious's every move.

I'm telling you, that man has a good heart. Yvette had insisted again and again. *He's just been through a lot, I suppose.*

Andie wondered exactly what, when, and why. She'd even run a background check at headquarters, but his record was clear.

Yvette grew more serious. "I haven't managed to get much out of him, but I know he's lived alone for a long time. So, he needs to get out a little. You know, resocialization or whatever they call it."

Andie scowled. That was the term used for criminals preparing for release from jail. Was it appropriate in this case or way off the mark?

Off the mark, Andie imagined her father insisting. He'd always seen the best in everyone.

"Plus, I have to meet someone tonight, and Roy needs something to do," Yvette finished.

"He has things to do at the ranch," Andie pointed out.

Yvette snorted. "On a Friday night?" She shook her head. "The poor guy needs to get used to civilization again."

Andie made a face. As a run-down bar on the edge of town, the Lone Wolf didn't exactly qualify as civilization. Not like the Blue Moon Saloon or other places in the center of town.

She pulled Yvette closer. "Roy nearly ended up in jail. He needs positive influences, not a bunch of strangers hanging around a bar."

Yvette patted her hand. "That's why I brought him here. You can keep an eye on him."

That's what we do, Andie remembered her father saying. *Not just as police. Everyone needs to keep an eye out for each other and be ready to help when we can.*

Still, Andie shook her head. "I'm working." *Or trying to,* she nearly added as a customer motioned for another drink. "Why can't you keep an eye on him?"

"That was the plan, but I got a call." Yvette's expression went all sly, and she glanced from side to side before dropping her voice. "I have an idea how we can stop the Lazy Q from being covered with McMansions."

Andie narrowed her eyes. What was Yvette up to now?

"Anyway, I have to go," Yvette finished, already heading for the door. Three steps later, she turned and called out in her usual breezy voice, "Be a sweetheart and give Roy a ride home, okay?"

With that, she ducked out the front door before Andie could protest.

"Two drafts, one Jim Beam," Carla murmured on her way to the kitchen.

Andie took a long, slow breath, then forced herself back to work. That included checking on everyone at the bar, right down to Cowboy Scrumptious.

"Hi," she murmured, wiping away the wet rings on the bar.

"Hi," Roy whispered.

One little word, yet it sent tingles up and down her spine. The same thing had been happening all week. Every time she drove past Roy, she'd offered a stilted wave or curt greeting. It felt awkward as hell with a guy she'd come close to arresting, but it was only polite, right?

But over the week, her gestures and words had grown warmer. Roy's reaction changed too, gradually going from serious and tight-lipped to flashing tiny smiles. Tiny, yet from the heart and packed with power to make her pulse race.

She reached for the empty glass left by the previous customer. Roy nudged it toward her at the same time, and their hands brushed. Just barely, but whoa. Even that little contact made her soul flutter like a hyperactive hummingbird.

"Sorry," she murmured, though it might have been a lie. "What would you like?"

His face didn't yield a hint of emotion, though his eyes sparkled. And, dang. Andie might have gotten a little mesmerized by that effect, because the next thing she was aware of — other than Roy — was Rita clearing her throat from the other end of the bar.

"Um, Andie? Should I get these drinks, or will you?"

Andie blinked. Drinks? What drinks? Then she spotted a large party of new arrivals and covered up with a nod. "I'm on it."

Only about ten percent of her focus went to drinks, though. The rest went to spying on Roy from the corner of her eye. He sat quietly, nostrils flaring as if he could smell every damn drink in the bar.

And, oops. Ten percent focus wasn't quite enough, as Andie discovered when Rita came by with a spare draft and a look that said, *What's up with you?*

Andie asked herself the same thing. What was so mesmerizing about her mystery man that she couldn't drag her senses away from him? And who was it he reminded her of?

"Hey, if you're not going to get Hot Stuff's order, I'm happy to," Carla volunteered.

Rita looked between Andie and Roy, then winked. "You know what they say about really living life. You have to let your fears go."

Andie kept her lips in a straight line. Fears? She didn't have any fears.

Okay, except maybe about opening her heart.

She put on her most businesslike look, grabbed a draft and a water, and headed toward Roy.

"What'll it be?" She held up both drinks, then arched her eyebrow in challenge. According to Yvette, the man was Mr. Clean. But was he, really?

After a moment's confusion, his eyes darted between the glasses. "Water. Please."

As usual, his speech was a little stilted, like a man who'd gone without words for a very long time.

She placed it before him, then stuck both hands on the bar, doing her best to channel no-nonsense bartender vibes. "Also, you're staring."

His Adam's apple bobbed, and he looked down. Dammit, how did a big, tough, *been out in the wild a little too long* cowboy type manage to look so sweet and so lost at the same time?

"Sorry," he murmured. But a moment later, his eyes bounced back to hers, and her breath caught all over again.

Finally, Roy tore his gaze away. "Sorry again."

Was he? Was she?

Her elbow bumped the checkers board left in the spot next to his, making a red piece slide. She slid it back, and then, on a whim, slid it into a new square.

"There. Your turn."

She went back to work, leaving him to contemplate the board. A few minutes later, she checked in again.

"Still deciding on a move?" she asked as Roy frowned at the board. "You're black, you know."

Haltingly, he slid a piece into a square in striking distance of hers.

She pushed it back. "Oh no, you don't. Letting me win will not get you free drinks. Try again, buster."

With that, she headed back to ring up a customer.

The next time she checked in on Roy, the creases on his brow had grown deeper. Slowly, he moved the same piece in a different direction.

She laughed. "Come on. Don't pretend you don't know the rules."

And, oops. He looked as crestfallen as a kid cut from the Little League team.

Yvette's words echoed through her mind. *He's lived out in the desert for a long time.*

Andie bit her lip, wondering how long… and why.

"Okay, look." She reset the board. "You can only move diagonally, like this, and only one square at a time. And you can only go forward. You capture the other guy's pieces by jumping them, like this. You can even double jump."

Click. Click. She moved a piece to demonstrate, then moved it back.

"Okay? I'll start." She moved a piece, then headed away again, figuring she would deal with queens when the time came.

"Your move," she called over her shoulder, hoping he'd understood.

Still. A grown man who didn't know how to play checkers?

On the other hand, who was she to judge? The couple of words she'd exchanged with Roy were more conversation than she'd had in a long time, except for talking to Buck, of course.

She caught herself glancing at the clock, then the door, longing for a wolf's company. When her gaze bounced back to Roy, she sighed. Longing for a total stranger, too? God, she was becoming as eccentric as Yvette.

Over the course of the next hour, business picked up enough that Andie barely got in another four checkers moves. Rita had barely sat down with a meal for her son, Mick, when the cook called for help with the rush of orders.

"Dammit," Rita muttered, then smoothed a hand over her son's cheek. "I'll be right back, kiddo."

Mick's reply was a little garbled, but his voice had that same patient, *We can do this* tone his mother's did.

And if Andie needed a reminder to get real about life, that was it. Mick was about her age, but he sat in a wheelchair, and his fingers, like the rest of his limbs, were bent tightly by cerebral palsy — a pretty severe case. Enough to make his no-good father give up and leave when Mick was a kid. Rita had gotten by through the years, but that didn't stop Andie's heart from aching when they'd first met, two years ago.

So, dang. Andie longed to dart out and help Mick, but business was too brisk. A bolstering smile was the best she could do.

"Hang in there, Mick."

She hurried through the next drink order and the next and the next. The latter was for a new arrival seated at the far end of the bar. Andie stopped in her tracks, making foam spill over the rim of the glass. The checkers had been pushed aside, and Roy's water was gone — as was Roy. A stranger had taken his place and was already chatting with the next guy, who was pointing out a news story on his phone.

"Some say it's some kind of big bird, but how crazy is that? It's gotta be a skinwalker!"

Andie rolled her eyes. Not that again.

She squinted and looked around. Damn, damn, damn. She was supposed to be keeping an eye on Roy. Where was he?

Then her gaze moved to a spot behind the new arrival, and her breath caught.

Roy was sitting at Mick's table, carefully lifting a fork to Mick's mouth. Once. Twice. Three times, waiting patiently as Mick worked down every bite. Every so often, Roy would show Mick a napkin and wait for his okay. Then he would dab the man's mouth and get the next forkful ready to go.

Andie blinked. It had taken her ages to learn Mick's signals — a twitch of the cheek here, a narrowing of the eyes there, or a jerky swipe at the air.

But, damn. There was Roy, switching from the fork to Mick's drink on tiny cues few would recognize or even bother trying to.

Mick sipped, then turned his attention to the football game on the big-screen TV. Roy did the same. After Mick snorted at a fumble, Roy raised the fork again, offering another bite. A simple process, really, but one that took time. Patience. Compassion.

Andie's heart thumped like the biggest, deepest bass drum, and Yvette's words echoed in her mind. *I'm telling you, that man has a good heart.*

Andie nodded slowly. He certainly did. Then she chuckled to herself, thinking, *They both do. Roy and Mick.*

Something rustled by her elbow then went still. She looked over to find Rita gazing in the same direction.

A run-down country bar on a Friday night was not the time or place one usually stopped to soak in the sheer beauty of the world, but for the briefest of moments, that was all either of them did.

"Well, bless his soul," Rita murmured.

Then she cleared her throat and hurried off, delivering three hamburgers to table six.

That pushed Andie back into motion too, but the warm, fuzzy sensation stayed with her for the rest of the night. As a person constantly exposed to the worst in people, it helped to see the best. Enough to reinforce what her dad had always said. *For all the bad in the world, the good wins out. You'll see.*

Andie focused on that, filling her soul with stolen glances at Roy and Mick for the rest of the night.

Chapter Eleven

Bars were strange places. Roy vaguely remembered being in a few, and they'd all been loud, gritty, and crowded.

Still, none were quite like this one. Here, the noise and commotion ebbed and flowed, broken by intervals of peace almost as profound as he'd found out in the desert. A man just had to pay attention to the details, that was all.

Most of those peaceful moments came when Andie approached. Every time, their eyes would lock, his heart would thump a little harder, and everything else faded away. Everything but the feeling that one plus one made more than two. Like they belonged together. Forever.

Yeah, peace was a good word for that, even if it was short-lived.

There was peace to be found with Mick, too — yes, Mick, if he'd overheard the name right. Mick didn't say much, and his hands didn't work the way most people's did. But Roy could relate to that, having spent a lot of time with clumsy paws instead of fingers. Try opening a jar or a gate with those.

Of course, the rest of Mick didn't work the same as most people's bodies did either. Still, it didn't take much to figure out what he needed. You just had to pay attention to the way Mick flicked his fingers or moved his eyes.

Plus, Roy could use some practice with a fork and knife. But mostly, it was nice to have some company without having to force conversation. They could just sit in amiable silence and create a little pocket of peace that way. Heck, maybe they could even play checkers sometime.

The big boss — a stout lady with a stern voice and stiff back — came by with a helping of nuggets and a drink.

"For you, mister," she said. "I reckon Mick is still working on his. Aren't you, honey?" Her tone changed on those last few words, going from pure business to pure love.

And, heck. For a minute there, Roy heard his own mother's voice, way back when. Before things had gone downhill. For her, for him, and for his younger brother.

Raymond, he nearly whispered into his glass.

Memories looped through his mind in a painful reel. Finding, then holding Raymond's broken body at the base of the cliff, wishing it weren't true. Hearing his mother's tears turn to incoherent mumbles as she took to the bottle again. Feeling his own hollow footsteps as he avoided those *Poor you* expressions everyone wore.

He winced at the echo of his mother's cry. *Why weren't you looking out for your younger brother?*

Why weren't you? Part of him wanted to yell. *Why didn't you ever do things for us the way other moms did?*

Instead, he'd taken to spending more and more time in wolf form. Drifting away from that roller-coaster life and into a new one. A simpler, more carefree existence on his own.

Just an existence, the back of his mind warned. *Not living. Not really.*

He gripped his glass harder, then glanced over at Rita — living proof that even the toughest circumstances didn't stop most moms from lovingly caring for their kids. Then he looked at Andie, who proved that hope could prevail over the worst tendencies of mankind.

A little of the bitterness in his soul faded, making space for better things.

He rotated his glass, staring at the wet stains it left. Was he really ready to trust destiny to deliver good rather than bad?

Maybe he could, because the evening passed with a lot less turmoil than he'd expected back in that gut-dropping moment when Yvette announced she was bringing him to a bar. If it hadn't been for Andie, he would have balked at the threshold. But with Andie there... Well, yeah. He'd found some peace — and maybe even a new friend.

And when Andie cleared her throat and murmured to him a couple of hours later, his heart beat in triple time.

"I'll be finishing up soon. Yvette said you could use a ride home."

His inner wolf was so excited, he barely managed a strangled, "Yes, please."

Soon must have been relative, because it was forty-five minutes before the bar finally closed. Once Andie finished tidying up, she ducked into the back room, emerging a second later with her keys and jacket.

Roy's heart skipped wildly, because he got to leave with her.

"Bye, Rita. Bye, Carla." Andie waved. "See you soon."

"Thank you, honey. And you take care, Roy." Rita waggled her fingers. "You're welcome back any time."

Roy wasn't sure what to say, so he nodded, then turned to Mick.

"Thanks for the company. See you later?"

Mick's lips curled up, and he uttered his reply. *See you later.*

"Bye, Mick," Andie called, heading for the door.

Roy followed her out into the crisp night air. He stood still for a moment, just breathing it in. Somehow, he'd gotten used to the stuffy air inside, but now that he was outside, he closed his eyes and soaked in the cool, clean air.

Andie paused too, and for a moment, it was just like those evenings they shared by her boulder. Except now, they were both in human form.

The silence was so pure, so sweet, that Roy wondered if Andie felt it too. That this was a natural extension of the time they'd already spent together, with much more to come, or so he hoped.

A lifetime, his wolf whispered.

Andie shuffled, and when he opened his eyes, she was looking at him.

"I swear I know you from somewhere," she whispered.

He swallowed hard. How to reply?

"I swear I know you too," he finally said, though what he really meant was, *I know we've met — often — and I think, deep down, you know it too.*

The breeze played with Andie's long hair, and he longed to play with it too. Her gaze lifted enough to make him wonder if she was imagining running her fingers through his hair. Then his blood heated, because her focus dropped to his lips.

The world went a little blurry except for her. He could feel it already — how soft that kiss would be. How sweet. How perfect. All they needed was to lean in a little and—

The bar door burst open, and two men stumbled out, laughing loudly.

Andie stepped away and cleared her throat. "My pickup is over there. The silver Toyota."

Her voice was back to all business, though he was pretty sure he caught a slight waver in there. Was she as keyed up as he was?

Soon, they were rolling down the highway with the windows cracked open to let the night air whip away the bar smells clinging to their clothes.

"Thank you," Andie murmured out of nowhere.

He blinked at her, confused.

"For sitting with Mick. It meant a lot to Rita, and I bet Mick enjoyed it too," she said.

Roy blinked again. Why thank him for staying in the only peaceful spot in that bar?

Andie swung the car around a tight corner, leaving the highway for the quiet ranch road. The rumble of tires over gravel grew, providing a lulling background sound.

"How's work?" Andie asked. "So far, so good?"

He nodded. "So far, so good."

"What about Brady? Is he treating you okay?"

He shrugged. If *okay* meant *with dignity and respect*, then no. Brady wasn't capable of such things. On the other hand, after barking out orders, Brady usually left Roy alone to execute them. So that part was okay.

"Fine," he murmured.

Andie turned the next corner then scowled at the billboard beside the road.

Lazy Q Ranch, it declared in huge, saloon-style lettering. Under that, in smaller print, stood *Secure your own parcel of paradise,* and at the bottom, *1-5 acre homesteads in the heart of prime Arizona wilderness.*

That was just the original writing, though. Someone had spray-painted over that, leaving oozing red letters that warned, *Skinwalker territory. Enter at your own risk.*

"Skinwalker. Again," Andie muttered.

He held his breath, waiting for more, but Andie just drove on, looking gloomy.

"Do you believe in them?" he asked.

She glanced over. "Skinwalkers?"

When he nodded, Andie scowled at the road for a while.

"I believe in evidence," she finally declared. Her eyes swept over the landscape, and her lips pursed before she went on. "But I've spent enough time out here to know that indigenous folks knew a hell of a lot we still haven't learned." Her voice dropped to a reverent whisper. "They still do, but most people don't bother to listen." Then she tightened her grip on the steering wheel and straightened. "Still, I find other explanations more plausible in this case."

He tilted his head. "Like what?"

"Like that cassowary that's on the loose. That could be what mauled the goats."

Roy had overheard the cassowary story, but he doubted a big bird, no matter how fierce, would have an aura as menacing and evil as he'd sensed that night.

"And the howling people have reported," Andie went on. "That could be coyotes. Or it's all just a hoax."

"A hoax?"

Andie nodded grimly. "Something set up by nature lovers to scare off potential buyers and keep the land wild — or even lies spread by the developers to attract free publicity." She sighed. "It's all trouble in the end." Then she rolled to a stop, looking up.

Roy looked too, and his wolf side sniffed. What was wrong?

Nothing, it seemed. Andie just leaned on the steering wheel and gazed at the stars. A faint smile played over her lips, and some of the tension eased out of her brow, leaving it less creased.

So beautiful out here, he imagined her saying.

He wagged his tail. Or — oops, no tail. Not in human form. But it did bring him back to those times by her boulder again. Just her, him, and the desert, stretching for miles ahead.

And just like that, his fantasies took off. He dreamed of bringing her to his favorite lookout point on the highest mesa around. Him and her, trotting side by side in wolf form. Then, at the top, they would settle down on their haunches, so close their sides touched. Close enough that when she lifted her chin and howled with him, he could feel the sound, not just hear it in his ears.

He swayed a little, just like he would when singing his part of their duet.

When Roy finally opened his eyes, Andie opened hers too, and for the space of a heartbeat, it was just like his fantasy. That little grin. That *Isn't the world beautiful?* shine in her eyes.

Then something snapped in the bushes, and they both whipped around.

"Jackrabbit," Andie muttered as a shadow darted through the scrub.

Roy sucked in a deep breath and hid the wolf claws that had started to emerge.

Shit. He'd let his guard down, and that wasn't good.

When Andie set the pickup in motion again, he stared straight ahead, reminding himself what he had to do. Track down the danger. Kill it or chase it away. Only then could he move on to step two of his plan — somehow winning Andie over and sharing the full truth. Ending the lie that Roy and Buck were two separate beings instead of one lonely soul.

"So, this is you," Andie murmured as she cruised to a stop by the turnoff to Lazy Q Ranch.

He glanced beyond her. The dim lights of the bunkhouse shone a quarter-mile down the track.

He'd spent a week there without minding the bare, basic nature of the bunkhouse. But suddenly, he was hit by an intense yearning to continue to Andie's place. Not for the creature comforts, but to stay with his mate.

Yes, his wolf side hummed. *Stay with my mate.*

Andie's throat bobbed, and he swore she was thinking the same thing, with her heart in her throat and her soul yearning so badly it hurt.

Stay with me, he imagined her whispering. *Take me home and fill that empty space.*

Andie's lips wavered for a moment, but then her chin jutted, exactly as it had that night she'd nearly arrested him.

"Good night, Roy."

Her voice was gentle but firm. He slid out of the pickup, chest aching, wolf howling inside.

You mean, "Good night, Buck," the beast whispered. *Please, say it, just once.*

He ached to tell her who and what he was. But how could he explain?

That wolf that keeps visiting you... That's me. I love you, Andie. I love you more than anything. More than I love the open range. And you know what? I think you love the same things... and maybe even me.

He gulped the words away, forcing his feet to carry him stiffly down the road.

"Good night," he called, determined not to look back.

He felt her eyes on him. Would she change her mind?

When she called out softly, he whirled, full of hope.

"Thank you." Her whisper came with a smile, and a little hope seeped into his soul again.

"No, thank you," he called softly.

Then he turned back to the bunkhouse and doubled his resolve. Maybe not now. Maybe not soon. But someday, somehow, he would win over his mate.

Chapter Twelve

To Roy's surprise, the evening he spent at the bar became the first of several more. Why? Well, the place wasn't as intolerable as he'd thought it would be. Not so much because he was getting used to human ways, but because he got to watch over Andie.

Of course, on most nights, he could do that by loping over to visit her at her boulder in wolf form. But having spent time with her as a human made him burn for more. The catch was, she didn't trust that part of him.

Yet, his inner wolf declared.

Compounding that was the uncomfortable sensation of lying to her, whether he was curled up at her feet in wolf form or sitting at a safe distance in the bar.

I'm Roy, but I'm Buck too, he wanted to say.

But could he ever utter those words?

All he could do was bide his time. And that was why, after another backbreaking day of work, he found himself at the Lone Wolf with Mick, staring blankly at the game on the big screen. Basketball this time.

As before, Yvette had dropped him off on her way somewhere else. The woman was suddenly busy with a new project of some kind, so instead of inviting him over to help her out in the evenings — her code for keeping an eye on him, he figured — Yvette dropped him off at the Lone Wolf whenever Andie had a shift. Then Yvette would rush off again on some secret mission she refused to reveal.

"I'm saving the ranch. You'll see," was all she ever said.

He had no idea what she meant, but okay. Even by human standards, Yvette was full of wacky, overcomplicated plans.

So, there he sat, turning his water glass, quietly studying everyone in the bar. Andie was behind the bar, her usual cool, efficient self, not taking any nonsense from any of the hard-talking cowboys at the bar. Every once in a while, her gaze would meet his, and his pulse would quicken as it always did.

You're staring, she'd said that first night, a week ago.

Yeah, he probably was, but when Andie caught him at it now, her lips rounded into a faint smile. He smiled too, but it faded when someone stepped between them, blocking their view.

He growled under his breath and went back to scanning the customers. No trouble in sight, but a sixth sense scratched at his mind, warning him.

Warning about what? he wanted to yell an hour later when it hadn't let up.

And, bam. Exactly then, the bar door opened, and a man stepped in, making Roy freeze.

His nostrils flared, and his inner wolf growled. *Stanton?*

No one else took notice, but Roy sure did. It was impossible not to notice another shifter stepping into his turf.

Yes, his turf. Even if the Lone Wolf wasn't *technically* his home ground, it sure felt like it by now.

The man's face was familiar, but different too, because Roy hadn't seen Stanton in years. He would have been happy never to see Stanton again, in fact. But there he was, beanpole tall, and if not as scrawny as before, then every bit as self-assured.

Stanton's storm-gray eyes drifted over the bar, then latched on to Roy. The hairs on the back of Roy's neck stood as if someone had aimed a gun between his eyes. Then those hairs stood even more, because Stanton grinned and sauntered over.

"Well, hello." Stanton plopped into a seat at the table Roy and Mick shared.

Not that Stanton acknowledged Mick. He did glance over, but it was more the way you might glance at one of those weird Picasso paintings where people's noses didn't line up with their eyes. A glance at an object, not a person or a living, breathing thing.

Roy squared his shoulders and leaned right, shielding Mick.

"Long time no see," Stanton went on.

The guy was a year or two younger than Roy, yet he carried himself like someone older, wiser, and higher up the totem pole. Stanton had always had that way about him — except around the Twin Moon pack alpha, old Tyrone, who never put up with any young fool strutting around.

And *young fool* was exactly what Stanton had been. Never satisfied, always stirring up trouble, but smart enough to make sure the blame fell on someone else.

Roy bristled. He'd been that *someone else* a couple of times. Him or his younger brother.

"You been doing good?" Stanton breezed on as if Roy had encouraged conversation instead of wishing him away.

When Rita hustled by and caught sight of Stanton, her motherly smile faded. Not an *I know you* kind of look, but an equally scalding *I know your type* one.

Roy scratched his brow. It made him sick to think that Rita — or worse, Andie — might assume he was friends with a guy like Stanton.

And, shit. Andie was looking over now, her eyes dark and narrow.

"I still think about your brother, you know," Stanton added nonchalantly. "A real shame. I miss the guy."

So do I, asshole, Roy nearly growled. *So do I.*

Instead, he let out a low, dangerous growl. "What are you doing here?"

Stanton either didn't get the hint or ignored it. He just grinned.

"Oh, you know. I happened to be in the neighborhood." Then he leaned back, signaled for the waitress, and went on in a slightly lower voice. "I hear Ty's in charge these days. Old man Tyrone finally retired — and about fucking time." Stanton chuckled. "I was thinking of paying them a visit, in fact."

Alarms went off in Roy's mind. Stanton had come dangerously close to being expelled from the pack several times. Maybe that had finally happened, sometime after Roy left. If so, Stanton wouldn't be welcomed back. And, despite Stanton's casual tone, the fire in his eyes said he was burning to challenge someone.

Someone like Ty, the new pack alpha?

Roy had never been tempted to return to Twin Moon Ranch. But even from afar, he'd gotten the sense that the pack had grown steadily stronger — and more peaceful. Apparently, Ty was doing a good job. So why rock the boat?

Stanton leaned closer. "What about you? You ever tempted to go back?"

Roy frowned. No. And never, ever in the way Stanton seemed to be hinting at now — to cause trouble.

Well, good luck with that. Ty Hawthorne was the powerful head of a powerful pack. Stanton couldn't touch them if he tried.

"Come on, I dare you to." Stanton grinned as if his stupid dares were part of all the good times they'd shared.

Except they weren't. Just another grim memory.

Carla, the waitress, stopped by before Roy could grit out a reply.

"What can I get you?"

Stanton flashed a toothy smile. "Devil's Springs vodka."

"Isn't that stuff like 160 proof?" Carla laughed and shook her head. "Nothing that strong here, man. The best I can do is a Stoli."

Stanton snorted. "That's half as strong."

Carla shrugged. "Well, that's what we got."

Stanton's face fell, and a dangerous glow shone in his eyes. The kind that said he didn't like hearing no.

Roy's eyes burned into Stanton's, now sure that the guy had been expelled from the pack. Then he growled a warning under his breath.

"Fine." Stanton dismissed Carla with a wave and turned back to Roy with an amused grin. "My, my. I don't remember you being so...so..." He searched for words in a sweeping glance of the bar, then stopped abruptly when he spotted Andie. "So passionate about anything."

The hair on Roy's arms thickened as his wolf rose toward the surface, and it was all he could do to keep the beast at bay.

A good thing Mick spoke up then. The words were slurred, but Roy caught the gist.

Stay cool, man, Mick was saying.

Roy flashed a smile at his friend and turned back to Stanton, who wore a look that said, *You're actually buddies with this guy? And what the hell did he say anyway?*

Roy snorted. Yes, he was friends with Mick. And as for what Mick had said...

Roy turned back to Stanton with a dark look.

Get off my turf, his inner wolf growled.

Stanton stood, wearing a grin that somehow implied that he was the boss, even though he was the one backing away.

"I'll take my drink over there, honey," he called to Carla.

She's not your honey, Roy nearly snarled.

Mick made a sound that had to mean the same thing, making Roy bristle more. Then he turned his back on Stanton and lifted his water glass to tap Mick's.

"Well, we told him," he declared.

Mick grinned wildly, then sipped when Roy raised the straw to his lips.

We sure did, his triumphant look said.

Chapter Thirteen

For the next half hour, Roy kept an eagle eye on Stanton as he drifted around the bar, joining folks at different tables or taking a stool beside a loner at the bar. Each time, Stanton stayed a while, grinning and talking loudly — loud enough for Roy to hear, if not make out individual words. Anyone he joined would start out chatting and laughing, but the mood gradually shifted until they were leaning close to each other, muttering and complaining about who knew what.

Gradually, the atmosphere in the bar darkened too. Instead of cheering the basketball game, customers jeered at every missed shot. Instead of easygoing chitchat about work, home, and play, they cursed taxes, city folk, and the weatherman. Rita emerged from the kitchen more often than ever, looking concerned. She and Andie exchanged looks a few times, then nodded in some kind of secret code.

Rita brightened the lighting, and Carla turned on a new soundtrack. The music still featured lonely cowboy tunes, but with less angst and more happy endings.

Roy kept his eyes on Stanton. Apparently, people never changed. The guy had always been one to stir up trouble and dissent.

Before long, heated arguments started cropping up. By then, Stanton was leaning on the wall by the old pinball machine, casually nursing a drink.

Roy frowned at a faint memory that surfaced out of nowhere. He'd seen Stanton flash that satisfied look before. But when? And why?

He gripped his glass a little tighter. That was the problem with all the time he'd spent in wolf form. Maybe it really had warped his sense of time and place. Over the past week, he'd often found himself leaning on a shovel or standing by a fence with no sense of how long he'd been there or why he'd come to that particular place. Other times, when he looked back on a day, it was filled with blanks, like he'd blotted out the when's, how's, and why's of what he'd done or where he'd been.

Now, he rubbed his chin, trying to pluck memories out of the haze. But on the opposite side of the bar, a man shoved his chair back, shouting. The men at the next table jumped up too, angry at their spilled drinks. One man out of six tried to calm the first guy, but the other five fueled the fire. Voices and fists were raised, and a moment later, a full-fledged fight broke out.

"Oh no, you don't." Rita rushed out, holding a tray like a shield.

Roy glanced toward Stanton, but the man was gone, and the front door swung closed, letting in a sliver of cold air.

In no time, the number of angry men grew to a dozen, and even the few peacemakers were drawn into the fray. Rita barked at them to stop, but despite her firm, football coach's voice, the fight spread.

A short time later, the first bottle flew, and glass shattered. A chair followed, and the place filled with shouts. A handful of customers rushed to the door like so many panicked sheep, but most remained, cheering on or joining the fight.

"Dammit," Andie muttered, snatching glasses and bottles out of their reach.

Roy jumped to his feet, ready to rush over and protect his mate. But Mick swung his arms and made a sound, making Roy freeze.

"Shit." He stood still, considering, then ducked as a bottle flew past.

His gut ordered him to defend Andie, but maybe old pack instincts were kicking in, because he couldn't bring himself to leave Mick's side. And what about Rita, out in the midst of the fray?

He eyed the distance to the bar. Wheeling Mick to the safety of the back room would be best, but the brawl had spread, blocking the way.

"Stop it! Now!" Andie boomed in her police officer's voice. She stood boldly at the edge of the brawl, hauling men apart and pushing others toward the door.

Roy gave himself a little nod. Clearly, his mate could take care of herself. He had to stay with Mick.

Easier said than done with the brawl surging ever closer. A chair came flying at his feet, and another bottle flew past his head.

Quickly, he moved the table and chairs to better shield Mick, then stood before that mini fortress, daring anyone to approach.

No one did — not directly, anyway. But two big, brawny guys shoved a third man, who tumbled at Roy's feet. Then the two followed up, charging at the guy. Roy lowered his shoulder, lifting and shoving one of the pair away.

Then another three guys rushed in. Fists flew, elbows jerked, and kicks landed with painful thuds. Roy delivered more than he received, but even then, he registered a few dull aches. That, and the sticky feel of blood dripping down his brow.

The main issue, though, was keeping his wolf side locked away.

Beat them. Kill them, his inner beast raged. *Protect my pack and my mate.*

Another attacker appeared, inches from his face. He threw up an arm to block the blow, but it never came. Instead, something flew through the air an inch away, distracting them both.

"What the hell?" the guy grunted.

Roy knocked him back with a punch that made his fist sting, then glanced back — and did a double take. Mick didn't look lost or terrified. He looked triumphant. When Roy spotted Mick grasping at another of the forks scattered across the table, he grinned.

"Thanks for covering my back, man."

With that, he turned back to the fight, and the whirlwind continued. Every time the brawl surged his way, he beat it back, barely restraining his inner beast.

"Stay away from him, man," one guy warned, backing away from Roy. "He's crazy."

Roy snorted. *He* was crazy, not them? How about the guys who surged forward every time he pushed away one wave of the messy brawl? They'd been stirred to such a fever pitch that they actually sought out the roughest parts of the fight. And apparently, that meant him.

They want a fight? They'll get one, his wolf side snarled.

Through it all, Andie pushed, kicked, or cajoled the brawlers away from the bar, where dozens of liquor bottles glittered, just begging to join the fight. The damage being done to the open area of the bar was nothing compared to the thousands of dollars of booze back there. But from the looks of it, Andie was holding her ground.

Of course she is, his wolf grinned.

Time jumped, the way it always did when things got intense, and Roy found himself grabbing a chair out of a brawler's hands. Just as he was about to smash it over the guy's head, a clap of thunder rocked the bar, and everyone froze.

"That's it," Rita hollered.

She brandished an old-timer shotgun, keeping it aimed above the heads of the crowd. A wisp of smoke drifted from the muzzle, promising she meant business.

"You men are a disgrace!"

And just like that, whatever evil had possessed the brawlers faded, leaving them looking sheepishly around in a daze.

"Now get the hell out of my bar!" Rita backed up the words with a menacing click-click of the rifle's bolt.

Andie backed her up with a look that could kill, and Roy let out a low, canine growl.

A couple of guys grumbled, and one shoved another. But for the most part, the spell was broken, and men started filing out of the bar. Some muttered under their breath, blaming anyone but themselves, while a handful truly looked chagrined.

"Sorry, Rita," one murmured. "I guess it got out of hand."

Rita fixed him with a merciless look. "You guess? Look at what you did to my bar!"

Wrecked chairs lay scattered across the floor. Tables were overturned. Beer and liquor pooled on the floor, aglitter with shards of glass that might have resembled diamonds if they hadn't been scattered over a scratched linoleum surface.

But Andie was okay, as was Mick, so thank goodness for that.

As the last of the rowdies left, Andie slammed the door shut with a *good riddance* bang. Still, when Rita rushed over to check on Mick, Roy didn't — couldn't — let his guard down. When he wiped his brow with the back of his hand, he stopped and studied the blood for a while.

His wolf sighed. *That's what we get from hanging around humans. Now do you remember why we left?*

He did, but one glance at Andie reminded him why he'd returned. And when she came over, eyes wide with concern, he knew he was exactly where he belonged.

"Whoa. Are you okay?" She cupped his cheek gently.

Despite the aches and pains starting to set in, and despite the havoc wreaked on the place, he smiled. One little touch from his destined mate and a blanket of peace fell over him, tucked in at the corners and cozy as could be.

Slowly, he raised a hand and touched her shoulder, praying she wouldn't turn away. When she didn't, the sense of peace went from a small blanket to an all-out sunburst. He couldn't get his lips to produce a sound, but he did whisper inside.

I am now, my mate.

Chapter Fourteen

Throughout the chaos of the brawl, Andie's heart rate hadn't gone above that of a slow jog. After all, remaining calm and collected was all part of police work.

But she sure hadn't expected her reaction to seeing Roy afterward. It was different to the fleeting glimpses of him she'd caught during the brawl, when Roy created a firm wall in front of Mick. Now, with the fighting over, she had time to breathe, and everything slowed down.

Everything but her heart, which suddenly leaped into her throat. Blood dripped from Roy's brow, streaking down his cheek and dripping onto his shirt.

It was all she could do not to run over and hold him close. Somehow, she'd managed to get a grip on herself and be halfway businesslike.

Whoa. Are you okay?

Now, that didn't sound too panicked, did it? And the way she cupped his cheek — that was just for a better view of his injuries, right?

Except her pulse was hammering, her throat dry, and her eyes suddenly burning with tears.

A good thing Rita stepped past then to thump Roy on the back. "I owe you one, son." After a moment of fussing over Mick, the older woman gazed around the wreckage of her bar and sighed. "Could be worse, I suppose."

Andie let out a barking laugh. "It could be raining?"

They'd chuckled over that old joke a hundred times, though Andie didn't feel much humor now. An inch more to one side, and the glass that had gashed Roy's brow would have hit his eye.

Her chest tightened, and she forced herself to take a deep breath. She'd responded to police calls involving all kinds of gory scenes. There was no reason for one little gash to hit her so hard.

"No, it could have been as bad as last time." Rita righted a chair, then slid in next to her son and forced a smile. "Thanks to you two, it wasn't. Thank you." She met Andie's eyes, then Roy's. "Thank you both."

Yes, Andie wanted to whisper to Roy. *Thank you.*

Chairs scraped as the last three customers started cleaning up the place — the trio of regulars who'd looked so chagrined. Roy moved to help, but Rita shook her head.

"Nuh-uh. Mick and I will oversee this crew. You, sonny, need to get cleaned up." Then she motioned at Andie. "Take him to the back room and put that first aid kit to work, all right?"

A dangerous zing went through Andie. Which was ridiculous. She wasn't a high school freshman crushing on a boy. She was a grown woman and a police officer who never let anyone or anything get to her.

Except Roy, maybe. Occasionally.

Okay, always. And right now, especially.

"Sure," she murmured, trying to sound casual.

Funny, how Roy's eyes seemed to glow. Really glow, like honey pouring through sunlight. But that was probably just an effect of the dangling light fixtures.

She led Roy away, slaloming around overturned tables and shattered glass. Then they passed through the kitchen and into the back room.

Roy pulled up short, gazing around.

"I know," she sighed, straightening a stack of paperwork that Rita called her Leaning Tower of Pisa. The place looked as though the brawl had spread this far.

"Rita's always trying to catch up, but... Well..." Andie trailed off there, letting the disarray speak for itself.

Pulling out a stool, she motioned for Roy to take a seat while she ducked into the bathroom for the first aid kit. Finally, she found the white box behind an industrial-sized package of toilet paper bigger than a suitcase.

"Got it," she said, trying to sound casual as she returned to Roy's side.

His eyes flickered to hers, then to the floor, and her sixth sense told her his heart was revving as fast as hers. Because, yikes. To clean him up, she would have to get close.

Nice and close, a low, distant voice rumbled in her mind.

She blinked away the notion that she could hear Roy's thoughts.

"Just tell me if it hurts." She leaned down to wipe the blood from his face with a warm, damp cloth.

He gave a tiny nod, though she knew it was a lie. Roy was one of those tough cowboy types who would endure a burst appendix before admitting to any pain.

She took a deep breath and ran the cloth along his chin. Absolutely, positively, not picturing what it would be like to do the same with her hand or her lips.

She gulped. No, not picturing that at all. No matter how sensual a ride that would be.

Instead, she followed his sharp jawline from one ear and down to the chin, then started up the other side. The light layer of stubble made it a bumpy ride, and oops — the cloth slipped, making her finger brush the softer skin of his cheek.

"Sorry," she murmured.

Dammit, her hand was as jittery as her voice, so she pulled away and covered up with a quick, "Oops. Still a little ruffled by the fight, I guess."

Another fib, but Roy didn't have to know that.

Or, shoot. Maybe he did, because that sparkle in his eye said, *Ruffled? You? Try again.*

But she *was* ruffled, dammit, which only made things worse. Her mind spun for some way to resist the pull she felt toward him. And she might have succeeded if her heart were in on the task instead of delighting at the prospect of something slightly dangerous and totally forbidden.

Why forbidden? part of her snipped.

A dozen possible comebacks swirled through her mind, but each was lamer than the last.

Forbidden because she'd nearly arrested him. But then again, he'd proven to be a good man. Darn.

Forbidden because she'd sworn off men. Except that had been back when she didn't want one.

Forbidden because they were only a few steps from an open doorway and folks who might see.

In spite of all that, she slipped deeper into a dreamlike state, as if destiny had hijacked her body and she was just observing from the back seat.

She slid closer and moved more slowly, motions that threatened to slip into *sensual massage* territory instead of first aid. Her arm brushed his, and her hair cascaded over her shoulder. Slowly, she pulled up a chair and sat close. Enticingly close, with her thigh touching his. His chest rose and fell with each breath, only inches away. And his lips...

She jerked away on the excuse of rinsing the washcloth. But even that tiny separation made her soul cry out, and she hurried back. Taking another deep breath, she started cleaning delicately around the gash.

A moment later, she stopped to scowl. "I hate that you're hurt, but when I think it could have been Mick..."

Roy's eyes darkened. "Humans are pretty terrible that way."

Funny, how alien he made *humans* sound.

She went on cleaning, then stopped. "What?"

He'd been looking at her. Right at her, with a question on his face.

Roy studied her a little longer, then finally spoke. "Don't you get tired of it?"

She waited. Tired of what?

He waved vaguely. "Seeing the worst in people, all the time. With your job, I mean."

His tone suggested *the worst* was the norm, and she sat back, considering.

Yes, her job sometimes left her jaded. Case in point — her libido lockdown, at least until Roy had come along. But on the whole...

She shook her head. "Sometimes, it takes the worst to bring out the best in people. At least, that's what my dad always said."

Roy looked a little blank, so she motioned toward the sound of sweeping brooms from the bar. "Like Evan and the other guys, helping Rita clean up. Or Carla — she was scared as hell, but she stood her ground." She paused, then whispered, "Like you, standing up for Mick."

Roy smiled. "Mick did his part too, you know."

She chuckled, picturing Mick clutching a fork like a dagger. "Like I said, bad things can bring out the best in people."

For the first time that night — or, wait. For the first time *ever*, she and Roy smiled openly at each other.

And, wow. The worst really could bring out the best in people, because his smile made her glow, warming not just her body but the frostiest parts of her soul.

Then she licked her lips in what might have been a Freudian slip and leaned in again. "Let's get this cleaned up."

She cleaned the blood from his brow, working slowly. Probably too slowly, but heck. She didn't want that wound to get infected, right? And if she got to inhale his clean, woodsy scent while she worked, well, that was just a fringe benefit.

When she'd started, Roy had kept his gaze glued to the floor. Now, she could feel it on her knee... Her arm... Even her face, at least in stolen moments that lit her up like a secret kiss.

Kiss...

Something she really shouldn't be thinking about at a time like this. But it was impossible to resist. Plus, there was something magical in the air. Something that erased the room's chaos and replaced it with the sensation of being in her favorite time and place.

An image drifted through her mind — one of herself and Buck at the boulder behind her house, with twinkling stars and comets flashing overhead.

Comets zipped through her blood, too, set off by a wilder side she hadn't felt in a long, long time.

Yes, this was a lot like that peaceful, comfortable feeling she got by the boulder with Buck. That feeling that she'd finally found someone to face the world with. A companion. Friend. Soul mate.

Lover, the naughty part of her mind whispered.

That was when she realized her thigh wasn't just brushing Roy's but inching between his knees. And, oh. Roy's hand had been clamped over his own leg, but now, it was resting on the side of her chair, close to her ribs.

Closer, part of her yearned. *Please. . .*

She continued her ministrations, but something else was taking over. Every move took on a sensual overtone, and her mind emptied itself of every thought but a few.

Lover. Closer. Please.

Before she knew it, her free hand was gently cupping Roy's cheek. Then, it wasn't the washcloth softly stroking his brow any more. It was her lips on his cheek.

The chair creaked as she slid forward, edging into his lap. A moment later, they kissed. A real, mouth-to-mouth kiss, as soft and full of promise as a birthday wish. Butterflies fluttered through her soul, and for the first time that evening, her heart rate slowed rather than sped up.

Roy slid his arms around her waist, and when their chests touched, the thump-thump-thump of her heart matched his. A low hum sounded in her ears, along with a faraway voice whispering, *Destiny.*

Destiny? More like insanity. What was she doing?

Somewhere in the blur that had smothered her senses, footsteps sounded. Just as smoothly as she and Roy had meshed, they slid apart again. By the time Rita stomped into the room, grabbed a dustpan, and stomped out again, they were back to nurse and patient. But their eyes remained locked, and their hearts beat as one.

Andie gulped, trying to play it cool. For years, she'd hidden her feelings from others — and maybe from herself, too. But now, she lowered her defenses. It was a slow, creaky process, like castle gates scraping open after decades of imprisonment behind rust and vines. But once she found a little momentum, a smile burst out of her, bright as the rising sun.

She smiled a little longer, then bit her lip. "It's not every day a bar brawl turns into a kiss, huh?"

Roy's lips curled, and he shook his head.

"It's not, but I'm glad it did."

She considered him a moment longer, wrestling with herself. Where to draw the boundary between *proper* and *desire*? How far did she dare venture from protecting to indulging herself?

Rita stomped back in, grabbed a trash bag, and stomped away, muttering, "Hell of a night."

Roy's eyes shone, and Andie nearly said, *Amen.*

In the end, she smiled and whispered the only words her muddled mind could conjure.

"Hell of a night."

Then she considered Roy a moment longer, and whoa. A few more words tumbled out on their own.

"I think it's time we headed home." A heartbeat later, she added in a whisper, "My place, I mean."

When his eyes sparkled, her insides did somersaults, picturing where the night could end.

Roy's shy smile spread another inch. "Yes, please."

Chapter Fifteen

Roy's pulse raced as Andie pushed the door to her house open. The dry scent of the chilis strung by the threshold wafted past him, balanced by the herby smell of lavender on the kitchen table. Then there was Andie's natural fragrance — a mixture of every desert flower, a little like the design on the handwoven rug on the floor. Every one of those impressions, he imprinted into his mind, because a dream was coming true. He was one step closer to *forever* with his mate.

Yes, it was just one small step out of thousands that stretched over rocky, dangerous terrain, but heck. He would take what he could get.

Dropping the keys on a table, Andie picked up where they'd left off outside — namely, by pressing him against the nearest wall and claiming his lips in a deep, hungry kiss. Desire coursed through him as their fingers tangled and their bodies meshed.

Mate, his wolf hummed in glee. *So good to finally touch my mate.*

Overwhelmingly good was more like it — literally, because all his self-control billowed away. Andie's too. Every inch of her body exuded a sensual vibe. She swept her tongue over his, marking him like a she-wolf marking her mate.

"This is crazy," she half whispered, half whimpered when they came up for air.

He shook his head, because it wasn't crazy. It was destiny. Which was a little like spending hard-earned money on a lottery ticket — a little foolhardy, but full of boundless possibilities.

"Maybe not so crazy," was all he managed before losing himself in another kiss.

If self-control was a wire with eight or nine strands, he was down to about four...three...two...

When Andie guided his hands higher to her breasts, the second-to-last strand shredded, leaving him hanging by a thread.

On the drive over, he'd been alarmed by the steady loss of control. Now, it thrilled him as much as the feel of her soft, supple flesh. Her scent was so rich, he nearly moaned.

But Andie beat him to it, tilting her head back.

"Yes..." Her voice was husky, her hands guiding his head lower...lower... "Right there..."

He got so lost in heady sensations that time skipped a little, as it sometimes did whenever he absolutely, totally focused on one thing. Like hunting in wolf form — it was that life-and-death, as if he would perish if he didn't succeed.

The next time he blinked into focus, things were turned around. Now, Andie was the one with her back to the wall, making sensual sounds as his lips worked her sensitive skin. He was pretty sure she'd been the one who pushed her bra aside, but he was definitely the one locking his lips over her tight bead.

"So good," she breathed, arching into him.

Every word, every touch made him throb with need. The need to make her howl with pleasure, and the need to do some howling of his own soon after.

So he kissed, licked, and kneaded until her breaths — and his — came in short, hard pants.

"Don't stop. Please don't stop," she breathed.

His inner wolf hummed. *Just getting started, my mate.*

Then she guided his head down her body, fanning the flames of mutual need.

Before he knew it, time had skipped again, and they were naked in bed. Not that the time in between was lost, just swirled together like a hazy dream. Roy was pretty sure he'd started out on top, but now, Andie was naked and straddling him, gazing down like a goddess of the moon or sun.

The moon, his wolf mumbled, registering the moonlight over the dim landscape outside.

Andie's face grew intent as she slid over him, and the moment their bodies locked...

Her deep, sensual sigh said it all as she sank down over him. When she tipped her chin up, he thought she would howl to the moon in raw pleasure. She didn't, but his animal side did, at least inside. Again and again as Andie took him ever deeper, tilting her head farther back and moaning with every hot, inner slide.

"So good..."

He was on fire, balanced on the razor's edge of pleasure and pain. But the moment he bottomed out inside her, it was all pleasure, and brilliant light filled his mind. And when Andie started rocking over him...

So good, he nearly groaned.

It wasn't just her hips moving. Her torso and shoulders followed in a sensual wave. She leaned back, announcing the perfect angle with a sharp cry. Then she went on rocking, demanding that he fill her again and again.

Waiting for the perfect moment to drive into her strained his last thread of self-control. But it was worth it, because if he timed it just right...

Ecstasy, a little voice groaned as lights danced in his head.

For the first time ever, he understood what the word meant. Andie was discovering it for the first time too, judging by the heady groan that escaped her lips.

More. He swore he heard her inner whimper. *Deeper.*

He was as deep as he could go at this angle, but if they rolled...

When they did, he bit back a howl, releasing a sharp hiss instead. Being on top gave him the leverage he needed to thrust even deeper, and when Andie wrapped her legs around him, his animal side roared. Then she clamped her hands around his ass, setting the pace for even more powerful thrusts.

For a short time, they maintained that perfect timing. But the higher they flew on that heady wave, the less important timing seemed. The universe started swirling around Roy, as if that bed was the center of a massive centrifuge, crushing him and Andie together until they had no choice but to become one.

One. Never, ever had one short word held so much emotion and need.

Roy gritted his teeth, then exploded with a low groan. Andie's cry hit a higher register, and for an instant, he imagined they were both howling at the moon.

Then time skipped one last time, and he found himself sweaty, limp, and panting hard.

Like logs glowing in a fireplace once the flames had burned away, their bodies radiated heat. Make that heat and sweet, sultry satisfaction. He slid his hands over Andie's back...her rear...her legs, clinging to that feeling of connection. His pulse gradually slowed, along with his breath, but his mind drifted happily in a haze.

It was only when he noticed Andie gazing at him, shaking her head, that his joyous bubble burst.

This was it. The moment her policewoman side went back on duty and realized this had all been a terrible mistake.

Her lips moved wordlessly, and a crack heralded the first painful fissure in Roy's heart.

But then she broke into a smile, and though she kept shaking her head, it was more in wonder than regret.

"What a night," she whispered, running a hand over his chest. Then she snuggled closer, mumbling sleepily, "What a night."

Roy took a deep breath. Holy hell. Yes. *What a night* was right.

Then he pulled a sheet over them both and kissed the top of her head, whispering, "Good night."

Chapter Sixteen

Andie woke up three times in the course of the night, and each time, things went the same way. The first thing she registered was a deep, abiding sense of peace. Then her eyes would flutter open along with memories, and shock would set in. That all-out, moaning orgasm — had that really been her? And that man she'd wrapped herself around like a boa — was that really Roy?

The more the sensual details fell into place, the more her mouth fell ajar. Had they really done that?

Yes, her vixen side all but purred. *Yes, yes, and yes.*

That really was her, arching in ecstasy and crying out to the rafters in glee. That really was Roy, driving her wild in his powerful yet tender way.

And, whoa. Not just that first time. The second time too, with her on all fours. The third time was up against the wall. Then came the fourth time, with her hunched, giving Roy head before crawling up his body and riding him like a cowgirl again.

So, wow. That really was her, glowing in satisfaction that went bone-deep.

Then her mind traveled further back in time, picturing the night she'd nearly arrested Roy. She sighed and stretched, sliding her leg against his. Now, the only person she was tempted to arrest was herself, because she lost all self-control around him.

Ha. Arrest myself for what? her vixen side teased. *Cardinal sin?*

Well, it did feel too good to be legal. Especially now, as their light, innocent touches took on an increasingly sensual overtone.

Arson? her vixen side chuckled.

Arson fit, because there was no way something could go from spark to full-out blaze so fast.

Nothing but the chemistry between us, Roy's glowing eyes said.

By then, the first rays of dawn were painting the sky, and the soft pink light played over Roy's bare skin. Both of them were stretched out, going at it in straight-up missionary style this time, oh-so civilized on the bed. But not exactly civilized, because something about Roy was wild and untamed, no matter how carefully he moved or how sweetly he held her afterward.

"Why do I have to remind myself it's okay to feel so good?" she whispered, half into the sheets.

Her lover wasn't much of a talker, but the few words he used hit the nail on the head.

"Because we're not used to it?"

We, not *you.* So, Roy felt it too — that feeling of an animal edging out into green pasture after life lived in a cage.

She ran her hand along his arm, then turned and kissed him. Gently first, then deeper. "Well, I sure could get used to this."

Her eyes drooped closed, and she hummed, slowly drifting back into a deep, peaceful sleep.

∞∞∞

The next time Andie woke, sunlight was streaming through the windows, and a meadowlark sang its two-part song. Her heart sang too, and she snuggled closer to Roy.

Then snuggled a little more, because there was too much space. A moment later, she stuck out her hand, searching.

Nothing. No one. No Roy.

She rolled over, looking around. Still no Roy. But her house was a small, two-room affair, so he couldn't have gone far. Her nose twitched, and a fantasy of him standing naked in the kitchen brewing coffee made her grin. Okay, that might not be Roy's style. Still, a girl could dream.

"Roy?"

Her voice echoed through the compact space. She sat up, clutching the blanket against the chill. Snow dusted the ground outside, but the cold went deeper than that. She stood, wrapping the blanket around her like a robe, and stepped to the living room. The edge of the blanket trailed along the floor, a little like her heart. Where was Roy?

Her spirits sank with every passing second. By the time she looked out the rear windows toward her boulder, pain and hurt were creeping into her soul. Buck and Roy were the only two souls she'd ever felt a connection to. But now, she was alone.

Then her cheek twitched, and some sixth sense made her turn to the front window — the one facing Lazy Q Ranch. It was as quiet a wintery scene as could be, yet something felt wrong.

Then her body stiffened, and her breath caught. That wasn't just the morning light. That was a set of flashing red-and-blue lights, and together, they stripped away the last vestiges of joy.

Five hurried minutes later, she'd rush-washed her face, finger-combed her hair, gone crazy with deodorant, and thrown on her plainest clothes — anything to cover up a night of spectacular sex. Then she jumped into the car and rushed over to the ranch. Her gut roiled, fearing the worst. What if Roy was somehow involved?

As things turned out, that wasn't the worst.

A short time later, she screeched to a halt and ran toward her colleagues — Officers Hanson, Lee, and Chavez. But halfway there, she halted and stared at the ground.

Blood. Everywhere. A trail of it, staining the soil from her feet all the way to the policemen and the grisly sight beyond.

Andie gulped and sidestepped onto unmarred ground.

"You remember Mr. Brady," Hanson murmured.

Her mouth went dry. Brady lay slumped beside an old cow trough. His eyes were open and vacant with death, and his gut was ripped out the way Andie had seen birds gutted by cats — though cats were neater in their work.

"Isn't this the guy who was pissed off at everyone last time we were here?" Lee asked.

"He still looks pissed off," Chavez muttered.

Andie had to give Chavez that one. Brady was keeping true to his nasty self, right to the end.

"Maybe this time he had a right to be pissed," Lee observed dryly.

Andie pursed her lips. Yes, she supposed he did.

She glanced in the direction of the bunkhouse, then jerked her eyes away again. Roy had been staying there. Had he returned early that morning? Had he seen anything or called in the crime?

Her hands formed fists as a sinking feeling set in. Surely, Roy would have called her before calling the police if he'd found Brady like this.

A plume of dust rose from the road as another vehicle approached. Her heart leaped, then plummeted, because it was Kyle, her duty partner. His civilian clothes showed he'd been off duty, just like her.

She nodded in grim greeting, then looked around, ordering herself to get into police mode. But now that Roy had unlocked all her hidden passions, emotion proved impossible to ignore. Where was he? Why had he left her bed so early? Was he in any way connected to this crime?

He can't be, she wanted to scream.

Kyle listened closely as Hanson described the little they knew.

"There are only a couple of ranch hands left, what with all the trouble lately," Hanson said. "One of them heard a noise, then called this in."

Andie looked around. Had that been Roy? If so, where was he now?

"He described it as *un grito animal* — an animal scream," Chavez chipped in.

Andie frowned. That sounded more like Jose than Roy.

"I'm not sure how reliable his description is, though. The guy is sure it was a skinwalker. Claims he was nearly a victim himself. He's barricaded himself inside the house. Arivera is trying to talk him out of there now."

"What do the other ranch hands say?" Kyle asked.

Lee looked at his notebook. "There are only two. Arivera is questioning a guy named Smitty now, but he drank so hard last night, he claims to have slept through everything. And judging by his breath, I believe him." Lee grimaced then checked his notebook again. "That leaves one other person we haven't been able to pin down yet — a guy named Rob Taylor."

Andie's heart missed its next beat, and she nearly whispered, *Roy.*

"Roy, not Rob," Kyle cut in, making Andie whip around. Did he know Roy?

Lee squinted at his notebook. "Right, Roy Taylor. Can't read my own writing. You know the guy?"

Kyle shrugged. "I know of him."

Andie gulped. Well, she knew Roy intimately, but what to say?

Lee consulted his notes again. "Apparently, he's a real loner."

That doesn't make him a criminal, Andie wanted to say.

"He appeared out of nowhere just a week or two ago," Hanson added.

Andie clenched and unclenched her fists. What to do? What to say?

"The thing is, those wounds look like an animal got him, not a person," Lee pointed out.

Chavez laughed. "Maybe it was a skinwalker."

Lee shrugged. "How about that cassowary? Or a wolf, maybe?"

Andie's heart leaped to her throat.

Lee squatted beside the body as the men muttered little details they observed. All but Kyle, who took a few steps away and turned in a slow circle, sniffing the air — one of the little idiosyncrasies Andie had grown used to over years of working with him. Then he stood still, staring toward the nearest ridge.

Andie followed his gaze, then froze, holding her breath.

Buck. Her lips moved, but thank goodness no sound came out.

The wolf peered down from the ridgeline, crouched and nearly indistinguishable from the landscape. If Andie hadn't been so familiar with the pattern of his dark fur, she would have missed him.

Her heart lifted, as it always did at the sight of her canine friend. But just as quickly, her heart sank.

What was the wolf doing there, now?

He seemed agitated, and what animal wouldn't be, given the lights of the squad cars and the body at the ranch? But most wild animals would run for the hills, not stick around to observe.

Go, Buck. Hide. Get away from this place, she wanted to yell.

But he didn't. Instead, he stared straight at Kyle.

Meanwhile, the other officers remained focused on the body.

"If it was a cassowary, it would have slashed his face, arms, or chest," Chavez was saying. "But the wounds there are minor."

Hanson paced closer, then scuffed the ground. "Tracks. Wolf tracks. Right here."

Andie would have turned to look if Buck hadn't swung his gaze to her just then. Her breath hitched, and her heart pounded.

Please, let it not be you, Buck. Please.

As if in reply, the wolf's tail drooped. *Don't you know me better than that?*

She did. Well, she thought she did. But she was starting to wonder if she could trust her own judgment any more. On Buck, on Roy... On so many things.

Lee went on, scratching his chin. "Not the kind of damage you'd see from a wolf, though. And the wolf tracks are faint, like it just kind of wandered by."

"Hell, maybe it really was a skinwalker," Chavez murmured.

"There are human tracks, too. Bare feet, of all things." Hanson pointed.

Andie paled as she recalled her rush to grab clothes a short time ago. Crap. Roy's shirt had been lying over hers. She'd nearly tripped over his pants on the way to the door, which meant he'd left naked.

None of it made sense.

She stared at Buck, sensing some connection there, yet unable to make the puzzle pieces fit.

Buck, she wanted to whisper. *Run away. Stay safe. And Roy, wherever you are, please, please promise you had nothing to do with this.*

Buck's eyes burned into hers, pleading his own case. So honest, so intelligent. So intense.

Her sixth sense kicked in, and she was suddenly aware of Kyle studying her. She tore her eyes away from Buck, then winced. It hurt. It actually hurt to turn away from the wolf. It hurt Buck too. She could sense it. But Kyle was staring, so what could she do?

She cleared her throat and fixed him with a *What are you looking at?* glare.

"Bare feet?" Hanson continued the separate conversation. "Could have been someone coming out of the bunkhouse to see what was going on."

"Or the murderer," Lee said.

Chavez snorted. "If a ranch hand wants to kill his boss, he's not going to do it like that."

Andie couldn't help but glance at the body, as did Kyle. For a moment, they contemplated the blood and the gore. Then Andie glanced back up at the ridgeline, just in time to see the wolf flick its ears.

Don't you trust me? he seemed to ask.

A lump formed in her throat, and she wanted to yell, *Of course I do!*

But should she? She wasn't a little girl any more, fantasizing that animals could be her friends.

Kyle shuffled beside her, making Buck bare his teeth. Then, with a last, mournful glance at Andie, the wolf turned and disappeared over the ridge.

Chapter Seventeen

Andie tore her gaze away from Buck before Kyle could notice. Too late?

Her partner cocked his head. He didn't utter a word, but his silence asked a dozen questions.

"Well, we need to find this missing ranch hand and check his alibi, if he has one," Hanson said.

Andie clenched her hands to hide the shake. *She* was Roy's alibi. But, God. To admit that now, to the men she worked with...

Still, it was the truth, and it could save Roy's skin.

She glanced back toward her house. Dammit, where was he?

Out of nowhere, Kyle grabbed her elbow and announced, "We'll check the main house."

She snatched back her arm and shot him a look that said, *We will?*

Kyle nodded firmly, heading into the homestead and down the central hall. The darkest part of the house and not the friendliest, what with the deer skulls, antlers, and animal pelts decorating the walls. Finally, Kyle led her out to the back porch and faced her.

She crossed her arms. "What?"

He waited without saying a word.

Three years of working with Kyle had taught her a lot about the man. He was honest. Quiet. Patient too, which gave him the ability to drag information out of people just by waiting with that *Don't mess with the law* look.

Well, two could play at that game. Andie crossed her arms more firmly and glared back.

Kyle glanced around as if to remind her they were out of earshot of the others, then finally said, "You know something."

She made sure not to show any reaction, but that itself probably tipped him off.

"Roy, the ranch hand..." he started.

"You said you know him," she said, turning the tables on Kyle.

"I only know of him."

"And what exactly do you know?" she demanded in a far too defensive tone.

Kyle paused, assembling his words the way a builder might lay out cement blocks that had to be placed exactly right.

"He lived on Twin Moon Ranch for a while. Before my time, though."

Andie's eyes went wide. She knew Kyle lived there, and she knew the reclusive, mysterious reputation of the place. In town, rumors flew, speculating that the ranch harbored everything from a religious cult to an organic commune. As far as she could tell, they were a decent, law-abiding bunch. She couldn't imagine Kyle mingling with anyone less.

But that Roy had lived there... She'd never guessed that.

"For a while?" she asked.

Kyle nodded. "About eight years, from the time he was fourteen."

"And?"

He went on slowly, reluctantly. "Nothing unusual. He had some tough times before, though, with his mom going through a couple of boyfriends..." Kyle's voice tightened, hinting at how those men had treated Roy. "The ranch helped her get herself together. And from what I hear, Roy was happy there. But then..."

Andie paled. "Then what?"

Kyle pursed his lips for a while before deciding what to say. "There was a tragedy." He stuck up a hand before she could drill him for more. "I don't know the details. All I know is he started drifting away and then took off entirely."

Andie thought of Roy the night she and Yvette had found him. So lost, so awkward, like a man who'd lived too long in the woods.

Then her thoughts skipped, sweeping over everything that had happened since the previous night, in what seemed like a different life. She gulped, remembering that first flash of bare skin she'd seen, and how much more she'd seen, touched, and kissed throughout the night.

Heat rose in her cheeks, and her voice came out all shaky. "Has he been to the ranch recently?"

Kyle shook his head. "No, but folks there would welcome him back." He glanced at the ridge Buck had disappeared over, then lowered his voice. "They're worried about him."

Her hands started shaking again. "Worried about what?"

Another long pause, then a strange answer. "That he's been out in the wild for too long, I guess."

"But he's been doing fine. Working here, coming to the bar—" The words tumbled out of her before she bit them back. Oops. "Yvette and I have been keeping an eye on him," she added a little lamely.

Kyle pursed his lips and, an eternity later, said, "No one wants to see him get in trouble, Andie. We just want to help."

His eyes bored into her.

Finally, her shoulders slumped, and she said it. "Roy didn't kill Brady. He couldn't have."

Kyle tilted his head in a way that asked, *And you know this because. . . ?*

She struggled to keep her eyes on Kyle's. "Roy was with me last night."

Kyle's eyebrows hitched, and a long, awkward silence ticked by.

"All night?" Kyle finally asked.

She nodded, staring at her feet.

"Until when?"

"Until this morning."

Kyle tapped his watch, asking what time.

And, shit. She didn't know. The last time she and Roy made love had been at about four a.m. When she'd woken up, it was past six.

That made two hours Roy had no alibi for. Plenty of time to get over to Lazy Q Ranch and kill Brady. But why would he?

Her mind spun, trying to weave a positive tale. Maybe Roy needed something from the bunkhouse. Maybe he'd gone over with the intention to return to her soon. But maybe he'd spotted Brady or Brady's murderer...

Maybe Roy was the murderer, Kyle's unrelenting look said.

"When did he leave, Andie?"

Her cheeks burned. "Sometime between four and six."

Kyle looked back over his shoulder, ensuring there was no one else there. "So, you can't be sure it wasn't him."

She wanted to stamp the ground and yell, *Of course I'm sure!* Roy wouldn't do such a thing. Seeing him with Mick proved as much. But evidence?

She had none.

"Where's the evidence it was him?" she demanded. "It's all circumstantial right now. Innocent until proven guilty, right?"

Kyle studied her for a long time, then let his eyes drift up to the hills.

"Right."

∞∞∞∞

Once the CSI team and forensic photographers arrived on the scene, Lee and Chavez headed off to further question Smitty, the ranch hand who claimed to have slept through the incident.

Andie spent almost an hour with Jose, being the only officer he would speak to. The man was terrified, jabbering half in Spanish, half in English while his hands flew, drawing crooked shapes in the air.

"Lucky and the other dogs went wild barking... I went out to check... When I came around the corner of the house, I saw it." His hands curled into claw shapes, and he pointed up. "Skinwalker."

Jose couldn't begin to suggest a timeline, only to wildly sculpt shapes that fluttered across the sky, then crept along the ground. Andie did her best to follow along, but none of it made sense.

Unless it really was a supernatural creature of some kind, an unsettled corner of her mind said.

Or just that cassowary, the more logical part filled in.

But the tracks around the house did as little as Jose to solve the mystery. The ground was so dry, no clear trail showed, just a blur of skid marks and dull scratches.

She glanced up, then shook her head. Nothing there, of course. Jose's terror was making him imagine creepy legends.

On the other hand, there'd been that night when she'd had her own scare. Those glowing, evil eyes... The knot of terror that had formed in her gut in the presence of whatever it was...

She studied the landscape, then headed back into the bunkhouse, where she helped Jose pack a few things. Then she saw him and Lucky off, heading for city relatives in a rattly pickup. She waved sadly, then stood there a long time after the vehicle disappeared around the bend. A dry breeze whispered over the rugged landscape, making the desert seem more desolate and lonely than before.

"Roy..." she whispered, turning in a slow circle. "Buck..."

All her friends had left her, it seemed.

She swallowed hard, then looked around. The desert was as beautiful as ever, and she'd moved there for solitude, right?

Still, her heart bled. Solitude could be inspiring, but it could be empty too. Especially after the special moments she'd shared with Roy and Buck.

Clouds crept in overhead, reminding her that solitude could have a dark side too.

"Officer Hale," Kyle called, breaking into her thoughts.

She turned quickly, hiding her mixed-up emotions. "Yes?"

"Shall we check in on your neighbor?"

She nodded, and together, they drove the short distance to Yvette's house.

"Brady's dead?" Yvette said in genuine surprise.

She had come out on the porch in a robe and fluffy, cat-shaped slippers, her hair in a morning mess. Then she shook her head with a sour look.

"Well, he had it coming. And you can put me on the record with that," she added defiantly. "That bastard antagonized everyone from Yavapai to Coconino County."

"Who exactly did he have it coming from?" Kyle asked.

Yvette snorted. "Where do I begin?" But then her demeanor changed. "Unless..." She studied them, then leaned in to whisper. "It was the skinwalker, wasn't it?"

Andie rolled her eyes. Further questioning revealed that Yvette hadn't actually seen or heard a thing, but that didn't make her any less sure about the skinwalker.

As for Yvette's alibi — a purely routine question, Kyle assured her — the artist broke out in laughter.

"Sadly, I don't have one, honey. I was home alone." Then she waggled her eyebrows. "Though not in my dreams."

Kyle blushed and strode away, muttering something about inspecting the area.

"Too bad I didn't have Officer Hot Stuff with me last night," Yvette sighed, watching Kyle go. "But I suppose he's happily hitched." Then she turned to Andie with a wink. "How's Cowboy Scrumptious?"

Andie nearly blurted something like, *I wish I knew. He left my bed sometime between four and six.*

Instead, she kept it short and neutral.

"Missing in action. And right now, he's suspect number one."

Yvette's eyes went wide. "No! It can't be." She swept her arm toward the police officers and yellow crime scene tape over at Lazy Q Ranch. "It was a skinwalker. Any fool could tell you that. Roy would never do anything that coldhearted."

Andie's heart squeezed. She wanted to believe that, but now, she wasn't so sure. According to Kyle, Roy had been away from civilization for years. A week or two of good behavior didn't mean he was totally adjusted and stable.

"Jose claims he had a near miss too," Andie added.

"What?" Yvette shrieked. "Jose? Is he all right?"

Andie nodded. "Scared to death but unhurt, I think."

Yvette was totally incensed. "Jose is a sweetheart. Why target him?" She started pacing and muttering to herself. "Poor Jose. Poor Roy. What a mess."

Andie turned to the hills. What a mess, indeed.

Further questioning didn't accomplish much, and not long after, Andie departed with Kyle. After a quick stop at home for a shower and her work clothes, she joined her fellow officers at headquarters in town.

She spent the rest of the day in a daze. Where was Roy? What about Buck? Those questions remained at the forefront of her mind, even as she spent the day investigating Brady and the ranch.

By afternoon, her investigation brought her to the Lone Wolf. Officers Arivera and Hanson had already come and gone, having questioned Rita, who was aghast.

"They made it sound like Roy was a suspect. How can that be?"

Mick was just as agitated at the idea, and Andie could do little to console either of them — or herself.

"I didn't tell them he left with you," Rita whispered as if another officer were in the next room. "What's the point if you just dropped him off on your way home?"

Andie nodded robotically.

Yes, her heart mourned. *What was the point?*

Was everything she shared with Roy a mistake?

Moving as if in a fog, she headed back to headquarters, where everyone convened to compare notes.

"Goddammit, has that exotic bird expert we called in still not arrived?" the lieutenant cursed.

"No, but the media has," another officer sighed. "They're all over the skinwalker story."

Chavez snorted. "Suddenly there's a story going around that the ranch is cursed and has been for centuries."

Lee shook his head. "It's almost like someone has been poking a beehive, just to make trouble."

And just like that, Andie pictured the guy at the Lone Wolf who'd spoken with Roy, then others, always in low, conspiratorial tones. The mood of the place had taken a nosedive over the course of the evening, and then the brawl had broken out.

She frowned, trying to think back. Had the mystery man stuck around, or had he left before the fight?

"Gentlemen, ladies," the lieutenant barked. "We need evidence. Leads. Not rumors." He shot a stern look around the room. "No other witnesses?"

Andie kept her lips sealed. Just hours ago, she'd been intertwined with Roy in the most intimate way possible. Now...

Kyle looked over, but she kept her eyes straight ahead. She hadn't made an official statement about Roy's whereabouts — yet. But what was the point if it didn't shed any light on the case? She didn't have an alibi for Roy, much as she wished she did.

Eventually, the briefing wound down, and Andie prepared to go home for the night.

"Hell of a day," Lee sighed, shutting his locker.

Andie nodded dumbly. Hell of a day was right.

Still, her mind insisted on turning over every piece of the puzzle, trying to make them fit.

"I say we go over to that artist's place and solve this whole thing," Chavez joked, then imitated Yvette's shrill tone. "It was a skinwalker. It had to be!" Then he went back to his normal voice. "That's good enough evidence, right?"

Andie nearly corrected him, because Yvette's words had actually been, *It was a skinwalker. Any fool could tell you that.*

Then she frowned. Wait a minute. At that point in the morning, neither Andie nor Kyle had described how brutally Brady had been mauled, and Yvette hadn't had a close look at the crime scene. So what made her so sure?

On the one hand, Yvette had subscribed to the skinwalker theory for so long, her mind was made up.

On the other hand... What if Yvette knew more than she'd let on?

Andie didn't want to believe it, but hell. She was a police officer, and she hadn't revealed everything she knew. Maybe Yvette had been the same.

Plus, Yvette despised Brady. That didn't give her grounds to murder the man, but it might make her hold back on something she knew.

Then hope bulldozed past logic, and Andie's heart leaped. Yvette had always had a soft spot for Roy. What if she had seen something that exonerated Roy? What if she was harboring him right now?

Andie rushed to grab her things and head to her car.

"Finally off duty?" Chavez called as she shoved the exit door open.

Outside, sunset painted the sky in shades of blood, and a wintery chill stole into her bones.

Andie hesitated.

Off duty? Yes and no. She had one more stop to make. At Yvette's.

Chapter Eighteen

The closer Andie drew to home, the tighter her hands clenched the steering wheel, listening to local radio stations' sensational reports.

"This just in from the skinwalker case..."

"The manhunt is on — if it's a man at all..."

"William Brady was well-known and well-liked..."

Andie snorted and clicked the radio off.

She peeked upward, hoping to spot the stars. That's what her father's advice had always been, and she could use a few points of hope and light. But brooding clouds shrouded the night, and there were no stars in sight.

Even the lights of her sparsely populated valley were dim. Over on Lazy Q Ranch, the main house, bunkhouse, and paddocks were mere shadows, totally unlit. Only the timer-controlled light by the ranch gate was on, illuminating a now-faded sign. *Lazy Q Ranch. Inquire within to buy your own slice of paradise.*

She pursed her lips and drove on. Her house was just as dim, with nothing but a couple of solar garden lights casting weak points of light.

Something registered in the corner of her eye, and she whipped her head toward the rise near her home.

"Buck..." she whispered, hoping beyond hope.

Her heart pounded, but it must have been wishful thinking, because a full minute of staring into the darkness didn't reveal anything. No Buck waiting for her by the boulder. No Roy sitting on her doorstep, ready to explain where he'd been and why he'd left.

At least the lights were on over at Yvette's, half a mile down the road. Andie continued in that direction, praying Yvette would have some news of Roy or at least some answers to the questions swirling in her mind.

"Yvette?" Andie thumped on the door a few minutes later.

No answer, which made her brow furrow even more.

She turned and scanned the property. "Yvette?"

Only crickets replied, along with the tremble of long-bladed grass in a growing breeze. A storm was brewing somewhere over the mountains. By morning, the peaks would probably be dusted in snow.

Andie drew her jacket more snugly around her body and approached the trailer in the yard. She hesitated, then called quietly.

"Roy?"

She wasn't expecting a reply, a fact made all the more painful by the silence of the night.

She went back to the house, knocked again, then tried the front door.

Locked. She frowned. Yvette never locked the door, not even when she went out.

Andie considered her options, then decided to go home. She was off duty, dammit. It was time to turn in for the night.

But when she drove home, parked, and stepped toward the house, something fluttered on the front door. Andie slowed, then plucked off the note tacked to the wood.

Must talk. Meet me at Bonfire Point tonight.

It wasn't signed, but the flowery script and artsy, handmade paper clearly identified Yvette. Andie stared at it, then out over the dark landscape.

Bonfire Point lay another mile up the road, a place not identified on any map. Why meet there? Why now?

Andie's pulse quickened. Maybe it had something to do with Roy. Maybe Yvette had convinced him to keep a low profile until the murder investigation focused on a different suspect.

Andie's gut churned. What if there was no other suspect?

She roared down the dirt road, her pickup protesting with every bump. Then she slowed for the final curve and pulled over next to a rusty Honda festooned with bumper stickers hollering political and environmental slogans. Yvette's.

Andie slid out of her vehicle, looked around, then headed up the bluff — the place Yvette built blazing bonfires on solstice and equinox nights. But tonight, there was no fire in sight. No one either, until Andie reached the bluff. There, a lone figure paced the narrow space, wrapped in a native shawl. One look at the dreadlocks poking out from that warm bundle told Andie it was Yvette. Still, she searched for a second figure, hoping to find Roy.

The moment Yvette spotted Andie, she rushed over and enveloped her in a woolly hug.

"Whew. You got my message."

Andie hugged her back, then extricated herself, wondering what next.

Yvette bit her lip. "I need your help. I think I might have made a terrible mistake."

Andie's eyes went wide. Yikes. Had Yvette killed Brady?

"I just wanted to help," Yvette insisted. "To stop the developers, you know?"

Andie nodded dumbly, not sure what to say.

"But it's all gone wrong." Yvette took Andie's hands. "I know who the murderer is, but I don't know how to turn him in without getting into trouble myself."

Andie's pulse hammered away. There was little relief in hearing Yvette hadn't killed Brady, because what if it was Roy?

It can't be Roy, her soul cried.

"If he finds out, he'll kill me," Yvette added.

Before Andie could utter a word, a twig snapped, and they both whirled to find a man two steps away.

"Shit." Yvette grabbed Andie's arm. "Stanton."

Andie peered into the darkness. The man was lean, wiry, and familiar. But how?

A wicked grin spread across his face. "Now, is that how you greet your business partner?"

"We're not partners," Yvette barked. "I brought you in to do one thing, and only one thing."

Andie raised her hands in a calming motion and spoke in her best cop voice. "Everyone take it easy."

Yvette stuck an accusing finger at the man. "You were only supposed to scare people off."

The man — Stanton — let out a barking laugh. "It worked, wouldn't you say? Even you're scared."

Yvette stuck up her chin. "I'm not scared of you. But that's not what I mean, and you know it. Brady is dead. Dead!"

Stanton shrugged. "You said to make things real."

"I said to make things *look* real, dammit. There's a difference," Yvette hissed.

"Is there?" he sneered. "You don't know the first thing about real. None of you do."

He was ranting, like some of the true *locos* Andie dealt with at times. The angry ones out to teach the world a lesson, although they'd lost their own grip on reality.

And, shit. Andie finally placed the man. He was the one who'd sowed discontent in the Lone Wolf, only to disappear before the brawl. A guy Roy seemed to know — and intensely dislike — judging by what she'd glimpsed.

Yvette shook her finger at the man. "Killing someone is not the same as scaring someone."

Stanton chuckled. "Ever heard of *scared to death?*"

Andie shook her head. Brady hadn't died of a heart attack. He'd been attacked so brutally, even some police officers were calling it an animal attack.

Or a skinwalker, as Chavez had said.

The bushes rustled, and two dim shapes crept closer, mere shadows in the night. Punctuating them were shiny canine eyes that watched her every move.

A chill went down Andie's spine. Dogs? Coyotes? Wolves?

Wolves, she decided, making out the thick muzzles and wide ears.

Yvette's eyes went wide in fear, but Stanton didn't so much as blink.

"Oh hello, boys," he called.

Andie gaped. Boys? She'd come across folks who fancied keeping wolves as pets, but most of those were half wolf, half dog, and few worked out. These two were the real deal — all wolf, no collars. No trace of tame anything, just a dangerous glint in their eyes.

In a way, they were a little like Buck, though nothing like Buck at all. Buck wasn't scary or menacing, but these wolves were. Not rabid, just cool and calculating, which was even worse.

At least they didn't advance. They stuck to the shadows, waiting for some command.

From Stanton? Andie eyed the man as her mind spun. Had he turned the wolves on Brady? But wolves didn't leave bladelike gashes the way a cassowary would.

Andie found herself eyeing the shadows, half expecting the missing bird to appear. But Stanton didn't seem to have one in his menagerie of thugs. At least there was that.

Andie glanced around, looking for a makeshift weapon or escape route. If she and Yvette could reach the cars, they would be safe — especially if Yvette still had that old shotgun in the back of her Toyota.

Andie turned sideways, trying to edge Yvette toward the trail. As she did, another shape appeared, and the wolves growled.

God, what now?

Andie stared into the darkness, then did a double take.

Her lips quivered. "Roy?"

It really was him, wearing nothing but a pair of jeans as if he'd rushed over from bed.

"Roy! Good to see you again!" Stanton grinned.

Roy scowled, while Andie went stiff. Nothing made sense to her, but Roy seemed to know what was going on, and that made her heart sink. Was he involved with Stanton?

Never, Roy's bitter expression said.

Then what? she wanted to yell. *Why did you leave? Where have you been?*

There was no time for questions, though. Not with the wolves snarling and showing their teeth.

Trust me, Roy's warm brown eyes said.

Andie wanted to. She really did. But that was her heart talking, not the rational side that kept her safe.

Trust me, Roy's expression begged.

Then Roy turned to Stanton, staring him down. Maybe staring down his own past, too.

"This stops here. It stops now," Roy hissed.

"Exactly what I had in mind."

Stanton turned his scheming eyes on Yvette, then Andie, making his intentions clear.

Andie straightened and channeled her toughest cop mode. *Oh no, you don't, asshole.*

"No," Roy growled. "No more. You've gone too far."

The brawl at the Lone Wolf flashed through Andie's mind. Roy looked the same then — all bristling, indignant power, ready to take a stand.

Stanton shook his head. "I thought you understood." He swept an arm over the open landscape. "This — all this — has to be saved." He scowled at Yvette. "You said it yourself. They had to be stopped."

Andie shook her head. It was always strange to realize that she and a ruthless murderer might have something in common. But that's what her father had always said.

Most criminals are ordinary people, a lot like you and me. It's just that they make bad decisions.

She could have snorted at that one. *Really bad decisions, Dad.*

Only a handful are truly beyond hope. That was another thing her father used to say.

Yeah, like Stanton, she grumbled to herself.

Yvette shook her head. "I want to save the land. But not with murder. They'll lock you up for life, you fool."

Andie touched Yvette's arm. This was not the time to get an unstable man like Stanton riled up.

"No one's locking me up!" Stanton shouted, flexing his fingers like claws. "No one tells me what to do."

Andie stared at the gesture. Claws... Cassowary... The open gashes on Brady's body...

Then she blinked, because Stanton advanced on Yvette in a way that said, *You're first.*

Roy stepped between them, sticking a hand out. "Stop, Stanton. Stop and think."

Stanton sneered at him. "Oh, I've thought this all through, believe me." His gaze flickered to Andie in a way that said, *Okay, I wasn't counting on having a cop here, but I can take care of that too.*

"Not another step," Roy warned.

Andie had handled enough fights to feel confident about subduing Stanton. Having Roy there made it two to one, and Stanton wasn't armed.

But that wasn't counting the wolves, who snarled and crept closer. How the hell did one de-escalate a situation involving wild beasts?

Stanton shook his head sadly. "I have to say, I'm disappointed, man. When you left Twin Moon Ranch..."

Andie whipped around to Roy, remembering what Kyle had said. *From what I hear, Roy was happy there. But then...*

Stanton's face lit up the way a kid might at a sports hero. "I wanted to be just like you." His voice grew gritty and vicious. "Saying to hell with everyone, you know?"

Roy frowned. "That's not why I left. I just needed some time alone."

Stanton nodded eagerly, like he was totally on the same page. "I get it, man. And now you're back to teach those bastards a lesson."

Andie's heart sank, but one glance at Roy assured her Stanton was only speaking for himself.

"I'm back because I want to be back." Roy's eyes slid to Andie, and *zing.* There it was — that inexplicable energy field that connected them. The one that promised, *I am meant for you, and you are meant for me.*

If it weren't for the circumstances, Andie might have reached for Roy's hand. But Stanton was on a roll now, and the wolves behind him growled louder.

"No one pushed me out," Roy told Stanton. "I wanted to go. And now, I'm ready to be back." His eyes flashed.

"Don't mix things up and call it revenge. Especially if whatever mistakes you made were your own."

And, *poof.* Any doubts Andie had about Roy vanished. He was a good man. Imperfect, maybe — like her — but a good man, willing to embrace his past with all its triumphs and mistakes.

Stanton, however, didn't seem ready to forgive or forget. He raised his hands, threatening Roy. Not with fists, just that weird clawing motion of his hands.

"I thought you were different, but you're as bad as the rest of them," Stanton snarled. "And, Christ. You're too damn soft. Just like that brother of yours."

Andie stared. Huh?

Roy's jaw clenched. "God, you're sick."

At the same time, he made a whisking motion behind his back, though it took Andie a moment to catch on. It was her chance to get Yvette to safety. But that meant abandoning Roy to hold off Stanton and two wolves on his own.

"Sick?" Stanton bellowed. "It's the world that's sick, not me!"

Andie's eyes went wide as anger twisted Stanton's features to the extreme. His nose grew more hooked, and his arms stretched to impossible lengths. His eyes blazed, literally going red, and sank deeper into his chiseled skull. All the time, his long, skinny fingers clawed the air.

"Skinwalker," Yvette gasped. "The real thing."

Andie edged backward, moving Yvette along. Not that again.

"You need to stop this now, Stanton," Roy snapped.

Stanton snarled. "No one tells me what to do. No one!"

He leaped at Roy, who made a last urgent motion to Andie.

She whirled, shooing Yvette down the slope. "Go! Get to the car! Now!"

Yvette took off, crashing through bushes and stumbling over scree.

Andie stooped to grab a rock as a weapon, then yelled to Yvette, who'd slowed to look back. "Go! Get home and call Kyle. Go now!"

Then she turned her attention back to the fight — and froze.

Roy and Stanton wrestled and traded blows while the wolves looked on, tongues lolling as if to cheer Stanton on. The thing was, it wasn't exactly Stanton any more.

"What the...?" Andie gaped.

Fur had speared out through his human skin. His facial features had stretched so horribly, she nearly looked away. Blunt fingers had transformed to razor-sharp talons and...

"God, no..." She shrank away.

But her own eyes told her the truth. Stanton was transforming from man to beast. Tufts of fur and feathers stuck out around his ears, and his face twisted into a horrible, beaked shape.

Then she gasped again, because Stanton wasn't the only one changing. Roy let out a growl as his back curved. Andie stared as his teeth extended into long ivory canines.

She froze as Roy's body transformed in the dim light. A lower, animal body, with four feet and a tail. A wolf, bigger and darker than those backing up Stanton.

A wolf she knew at first sight.

"Buck..." she whispered, dumb struck.

No. It wasn't possible. It couldn't be.

Roy — or was it Buck? — crashed into the creature Stanton had turned into. An instant later, when they sprang apart, Buck caught her eyes.

Don't be afraid. It's me. Roy. Buck.

Andie froze, unable to move, unable to think.

Then Stanton launched into a gravity-defying hop-jump, rising six feet into the air with a flutter of wings.

Andie stared. Wings? Wolves? Was she going crazy?

Just then, Yvette's shrill cry sounded from below. "Andie! Come on!"

Buck's look told her the same thing.

Andie resisted the wave of fear gripping her soul. But this was radically different from any mission she'd ever faced with the police. Finally, she surrendered to instinct and whirled, bushwhacking down the slope to where Yvette was waiting.

"Come on," Yvette said grimly. "Time to get the hell out of here."

Chapter Nineteen

Roy snarled, rising up on his rear paws to ward off Stanton's talons. He did — barely — then lunged forward, an instant too late to land a blow.

Skinwalker, Yvette had hissed.

No, but close enough, Roy figured. Back in the day, everyone on Twin Moon Ranch knew Stanton was some kind of mixed-breed shifter, though no one had asked any questions. It was enough to know that Stanton and his she-wolf mother were on the run from her violent ex-lover. Twin Moon Ranch was run by a harsh, old-school alpha back then, but even old Tyrone had an honor code. He'd granted Stanton and his mother safe harbor on the ranch, much like Roy's mother had been given back when Roy was a kid.

So, in a way, Stanton was right. They had a lot in common, from troubled childhoods to new lives at Twin Moon Ranch to leaving for a loner's life in the wild.

But boy, did the similarities end there.

Stanton's eyes glowed red with anger, even evil, as they circled, growling.

Oh, sorry. Didn't mean to scare your girlfriend, Stanton goaded him.

Roy bared his teeth. *Leave her out of this.*

Of course, Stanton didn't. *Great body. Is she as good in bed as she looks?* He licked his lips. *Now that would be something. Gives handcuffs a whole new purpose.* He cackled. *Didn't think you were the type, though.*

Roy snarled. *There's a lot you don't know about me.*

Stanton grinned. *And a lot you don't know about me, buddy.*

I know enough. I know you killed Brady.

That, Roy had to give him. He'd spent every spare minute of the past week patrolling the area, but he hadn't found a trace of trouble — until that morning. A beautiful morning a breath away from Andie, until an ominous feeling had made him sit up in a cold sweat. He'd gone out to investigate, but he hadn't been able to shift, because his wolf resisted.

Can't leave my mate. Won't!

But he had to, so he did, sprinting barefoot across the pre-dawn desert, where everything was deathly hushed except for two blood-curdling screams.

He'd been too late to save Brady, but not too late to witness Stanton taunting the dying man, then heading for Jose's bunkhouse on a mission to kill. Roy had cut Stanton off, but they'd both halted at the distant wail of sirens.

Stanton's eyes had glinted, apparently weighing up the joy of another killing versus the risk it posed now that the police were moving in. Finally, he'd grumbled and taken off in that bizarre flutter-fly-running motion of his.

Roy couldn't help but stop and stare. No one had ever asked Stanton what his father was, but eagle was Roy's guess.

More like vulture, his inner wolf grumbled.

Either way, a mixed-form shifter was rare. Most mixed breeds took a single animal form — whichever dominated their genes. The offspring of a wolf shifter mother and vulture father ought to shift into one or the other form, at least upon hitting puberty and starting to shift at all.

Stanton had just been entering that stage when Roy had left Twin Moon Ranch. Roy had assumed Stanton would become a wolf shifter, but the more he thought back, the more he realized Stanton had always slunk away to shift alone.

Now, it was clear why. Stanton was a cross-shifter — half wolf, half bird.

I know you're no skinwalker, Roy snarled now, facing his foe.

Stanton snorted. *I know and you know, but humans are so fucking stupid.*

The wolves flanking Stanton huffed in amusement.

Roy did his best to stay cool and buy Andie time to escape, but that would be tricky. The only good part of the situation was it proved he wasn't crazy or schizophrenic, as he'd worried lately. Worries like, what if there was no outside danger, just himself to blame for the troubles at the ranch? What if shifters who stayed too long in the wild really did lose their minds and turn rogue?

So, no. He wasn't going crazy. He had been right to stay close to Andie rather than forcing himself away.

Still, it had all led to this, and now Andie's life was on the line.

Last chance to cut your losses and run, Roy warned Stanton.

No one tells me what to do. Stanton's eyes blazed as he and Roy circled each other, both snarling like a couple of wild beasts.

Roy mourned, because that was what Andie believed him to be. As Buck, he'd always made sure to show the friendliest possible version of his canine self, all wagging tail, gentle moves, and not-too-obvious fangs. Now, he had to unleash his most terrifying, ferocious side.

It hurt, knowing that to save his true love, he would alienate her forever.

So, show her we love her. Prove what we'll do for her, once and for all, his wolf side growled. *Not just when it's easy, like on quiet, starry nights, but now, when everything is on the line.*

He took a deep breath, making a vow. He would stand his ground for the woman he loved. He would win her over or die trying.

He pulled his lips back another millimeter, growling at Stanton.

Like I said. This mess you started ends here.

This is just the beginning, Stanton cackled. *Don't you understand?*

Stanton's eyes glinted when he glanced in the direction of Twin Moon Ranch. Obviously Stanton had some kind of half-baked plan to return and stir up trouble, like he'd done at the bar. The guy had become a master of that game.

Why? Maybe because anger, protest, and disorder were the easy way out when things didn't go your way. Getting along, building consensus, and negotiating solutions, on the other hand — those were hard work.

Roy let out a slow breath, a little ashamed. Once upon a time, he'd taken the easy way out by leaving home. But like old Aunt Jean always said, it was never too late to set things straight.

He gulped. Or try, at least.

He squared his shoulders and glared at Stanton.

This stops here. It stops now.

Stanton flashed a dangerous grin. *Oh yeah? Try me.*

That set off Stanton's next attack. And, shit. It was impossible to know where to focus. Stanton fluttered and clacked his talons a foot over Roy's head, while the wolves nipped at his flanks. Judging by the scent, both were shifters.

The only good news was that they focused on him, giving Andie a chance to escape.

A split second later, he yelped as Stanton's talon ripped down his back. The wound wasn't deep, but it stung like hell. He jumped up, snapping at Stanton, who laughed as he fluttered out of reach. The bizarre creature couldn't stay aloft for long, but Roy didn't have the luxury of timing his counterattacks, not with the wolves barging in at his sides.

He whirled, slashing with his claws and reaching with his fangs. One of the wolves yelped, and an acrid taste filled Roy's mouth.

Blood. The wolf's, not his.

The next minutes went by in a blur. With all his focus on the fight, Roy couldn't tell where Andie was until Stanton yelled at his men.

They're getting away. Kill them!

One of the wolves took off down the path, and Roy prayed Andie had enough of a head start to hustle Yvette to the car.

Talons sliced the air, aiming for Roy's eyes. He ducked, clamping his jaws around Stanton's leg before the wolf-bird beast could retreat. Roy twisted, hoping to throw Stanton to the ground and tear out his throat. But the second wolf sank its teeth into his flank just then, and his howl of pain allowed Stanton to break loose.

Dirt scattered as a free-for-all ensued, with Roy, Stanton, and the wolf all scrambling to break apart. Then a gunshot boomed through the night, and they all stopped.

Bang! Bang!

A second shot echoed over the hills, followed by eerie silence.

For a moment, Roy, Stanton, and the wolf all hung back, glaring at one another. Shifters were hard to kill, but even they couldn't survive a bullet aimed by a cool, expert markswoman.

Go, Andie! he nearly cheered.

Then an engine roared to life, and Stanton cursed under his breath. A vehicle sped away, scattering gravel. Roy's soul stirred with a mix of relief and sorrow. Andie was driving to safety, but she was leaving him. For good?

Roy's heart sank, while Stanton bared his teeth. Clearly, he was already working on a Plan B to eliminate those two witnesses to his evil deeds.

Roy growled. *Over my dead body.*

Be careful what you wish for, Stanton sneered, motioning to the cliffy side of the bluff. *I could push you off that, and you'd end up just like your brother.*

Roy's blood went cold. It wasn't just the mention of his brother — it was the knowing tone Stanton used.

If it's high enough, of course, Stanton added, making a show of peeking over the edge. *Not even shifter healing could fix you after a fall like that.*

Why the hell did Stanton seem so damned smug?

Then it hit him.

You were there, Roy growled. *You were there the night Raymond died.*

Stanton's wide grin said, *I wasn't just there, buddy.* Still, he stood silently, daring Roy to figure it out.

Roy's jaw dropped. Dares... Raymond... A tragic fall so long ago...

You made Raymond do it, he choked out in a canine snarl. *You made him fall.*

Stanton flashed the fakest *Who, me?* look ever and shrugged. *It wasn't my fault he decided to get too close to the edge. Not my fault it didn't hold.*

Roy's vision went red. Of course, Raymond had taken the dare. Anything to impress another kid and fit in. But venturing out to the edge hadn't been Raymond's idea any more than killing Brady had been Yvette's.

Stanton. It was always Stanton, stirring up trouble and letting others suffer the consequences.

Every muscle in Roy's body coiled, and his blood raged. He leaped into his next attack, and the world became a blur.

A painful blur, because for every direct hit he scored on Stanton or the wolf, they avenged, and his wounds were adding up.

Still, he gritted his teeth and fought on. For his brother. For Andie. For every decent person Stanton had ever hurt.

Blood dripped from his brow, stinging his right eye. He blinked because, damn. Now he was seeing things — like Andie, creeping up behind his attackers, hefting a rifle.

Which made no sense, because she'd escaped, right?

Then it hit him. Yvette had driven away, but Andie had backtracked up to the bluff, rifle firmly in hand.

Why? he wanted to yell. She was supposed to hurry to safety, not back into danger. *Why?*

Andie's hand looked a little shaky, but her expression was fierce, and two words ghosted through his mind.

For you.

His whole soul warmed. But when Andie raised the rifle and aimed directly at him, he froze, wanting to scream. To explain. He was a friend, not a foe. Her friend and lover, not a rabid animal.

Andie. . . he started.

But it was too late. Her finger closed on the trigger.

No! he wanted to yell. Dying would be okay, but Andie's fear would haunt him for all eternity.

No, his aching heart begged. *I love you. Please believe in me!*

But her finger was already squeezing the trigger, and all he could do was whimper one more time.

No!

Chapter Twenty

Andie's heart raced as she took aim. The shot she fired would take a life, and she knew it.

So make it the right life, she swore to herself.

There was no mistaking the dark-colored wolf staring at her with wide, brown eyes. Buck — er, Roy.

She halted one millimeter away from pulling the trigger, then yelled out in her best cop voice.

"Hold it right there!"

They wouldn't, and she knew it, but all she needed was for the light-colored wolf to edge away from Buck. She'd already figured out the hard way that Yvette's old Ruger 44 was a little out of true. That meant she had to aim a hair left of her target, and the slightest misjudgment could cost Buck his life. She wished for more of a buffer — and got it when Stanton's wolf whirled to face her.

She gave it another split second. If the beast showed the slightest hint of fear, regret, or retreat, she would spare its life. But the minute it narrowed its bloodthirsty eyes on her, she fired.

Boom!

The wolf dropped hard, dead.

Holy shit, Buck's wide eyes said.

Andie winced. Had he really thought she was aiming at him?

Never, she nearly swore aloud.

Swallowing hard, she swung the muzzle toward Stanton. It was one of those kill-or-be-killed moments every police officer dreaded, and she sure wasn't going to be the one to blink first.

But, yikes. It was one thing to face a wolf. Facing a bizarre, bird-wolf mix made her mind spin.

She yelled the only words that came to her tongue just then. "I said, hold it right there!"

Stanton snickered and leaped high into the air, then plunged down at Buck. Apparently, Stanton wasn't worried about being shot as long as he stayed close to Buck. That, or he'd counted how many rounds she'd used.

Are you nuts? Yvette had grabbed her arm when Andie had gotten herself together and refused to join Yvette in the car.

No, she wasn't nuts. She was a police officer, which meant she didn't run from problems. She solved them.

The rifle had made her plan slightly less suicidal, but still. Yvette had pointed out a critical detail.

The magazine only holds four. With that, Yvette started rooting through the glove compartment. An eternity passed before she fished out one more cartridge and pressed it into Andie's hand.

That left Andie with three rounds — and a mental note to give Yvette a long lecture about proper storage of weapons and ammunition...if she survived this nightmare.

She shuffled into a wider stance, keeping the rifle high, waiting for her chance.

Clearly, Stanton was not about to give in. Mauling Buck to death seemed more like his plan.

At least the fight was more balanced now. Stanton's angry screeches took on a more frustrated tone, and his movements became more desperate. Meanwhile, Buck fought with such bitterness and vengeance, she wondered what Stanton had said or done.

But blood stained much of Buck's fur, and the shine in his canine eyes grew a little duller. Andie swung the rifle muzzle around, tracking Stanton. She couldn't wait much longer, not with the way Buck was flagging.

Fading, instinct said, terrifying her. If she didn't do something soon, Buck would bleed to death.

Stanton must have come to the same realization, because his strategy shifted. Instead of all-out attacks, he harassed Buck, who had no choice but to fight back, expending precious energy.

Andie squinted and took a long, slow breath. No more waiting. In the split second when Stanton surged upward to avoid Buck's teeth, she fired.

Boom! Feathers flew, and Stanton hissed

Bitch, his furious expression said.

She'd hit one of his short, stubby wings, but not his torso. Andie was still cursing the rifle when Stanton flew at her.

In what seemed like slow motion, she heaved the rifle higher and squeezed the trigger.

Bang! Bang!

Her last two shots, and she had no idea if they were on target. Time, space, and sound all seemed to scramble, and she wasn't sure whether her mind registered every detail in order.

Buck roared nearby, and a pack of wolves howled in the distance.

Stanton screeched and swooped at her, his bulging eyes the color of blood.

Her own body was moving — ducking...falling...bruising against a rocky surface close to the cliff's edge. The rifle clattered away, then dropped over the cliff and banged several times on the way to the rocks far below.

She blinked, wondering if her father had experienced the same disjointed sensations before he'd died.

Stanton was only an inch away. A dozen self-defense moves flashed through her mind, but which suited a creature with claws and wings? In the end, she gouged at the red eyes glowing like windows to hell.

Then, *whack!* Stanton knocked into her with such force, her lungs emptied.

Andie! she swore she heard Roy's anguished voice in her mind.

Pain exploded throughout her body, but not the way she expected. There was no rip of razor-sharp talons, no plunging fangs. Just dull, all-over pain as she was dashed aside.

The screams that sounded a moment later weren't hers. That, or she was having one of those out-of-body experiences reported by people who'd died, then been revived.

When canine growls joined the screeches, she opened her eyes. And, whoa. Not even twelve years of police work prepared her for what she saw: a wolf and a bird-like beast locked in mortal combat.

Andie crab-walked back, then dead-ended against a boulder. Feathers flew, and the noise was deafening. Finally, the wolf clamped its jaws around Stanton's throat, ending the fight.

Andie closed her eyes to the ugly scene, only peeking when things went eerily silent. That made her just in time to see Buck give the limp body one more shake before heaving it off the cliff.

When a low thump sounded, she winced, then stared at her own feet.

Her heart hammered. Her breath came in pants, and her muscles cramped. Finally, she made herself look up. And, hell. Buck was a bloody mess.

For a moment, all she could do was stare. The only sounds were Buck's panting and the wind sweeping over the desert. Then she heard a whisper — her own voice, calling to him.

"Buck..."

She'd never seen the proud wolf look so forlorn or so weary. His eyes flicked to the ground, and his body drooped.

"Roy..." she said, more urgently.

Her heart squeezed. He probably thought she was terrified of him.

And truthfully, she was terrified. But not so much of Buck as of the stark reality facing her now.

Skinwalkers. Werewolves. Supernatural beings. They really did exist.

Slowly, she crawled toward him. Buck — Roy — had proven himself to her again and again. It was time she proved herself to him.

"Buck!" She rushed forward as the wolf swayed and fell.

Her mind spun with snippets of first aid training, police protocols, and sheer panic. What if Buck died?

Desperately, she smoothed her hands over him. But how the hell did one stanch bleeding on a canine?

"Please. . ." she whispered, as helpless as the average witness in a first responder case. As a police officer, she knew how to keep a cool head. But Buck — and Roy — were too close to her heart for her to keep a cool anything.

"Please tell me you're okay," she begged. *Please don't die,* she nearly added. *Please survive, so you can explain all this to me, and so I can explain what you mean to me.*

But she couldn't articulate any of that. All she could do was hug him and beg.

"Please. . . please. . ."

She knew damned well that begging didn't dissuade the hard heart of destiny. But she couldn't help it.

"Please. . ."

The wolf's chest had been rising and falling in heavy breaths, and when they slowed, she panicked. But *slow* didn't peter out to *stop*, thank goodness. Instead, his breaths grew longer and steadier. The furry bulk beneath her shuffled gingerly, finding a new position. Buck slid his muzzle into her lap, then closed his eyes, only to peek up a moment later.

Only then did it dawn on her how careful Buck had been not to scare her — not now, and not before, when they'd met by the boulder near her home.

A split second later, another realization struck her. She knew his fear all too well. The fear of opening up, of truly trusting someone.

She leaned over Buck, hugging him as tightly as she dared. *I'm letting my fears go,* she let the hug say. *It might take a while, but I promise I'll get there.*

Then she swallowed and put it into a whisper. "Please stay with me. Please be okay. Please give me a chance." It all came out in a rush, then one last choked whisper. "Please."

Then she giggled — yes, giggled, because he licked her cheek.

Buck licked her a second time, returning her promise.

I'm letting my fears go too. It might take a while, but I promise I'll get there with you.

How long they stayed that way, Andie had no idea. But eventually, tense silence gave way to a peaceful night filled with reassuring, normal sounds. The whisper of the breeze over scrubby mesas. The chorus of crickets chirping. The pinprick lights of stars peeking out between cloudy patches, promising everything would be all right.

Andie shivered, registering the cold for the first time. Then she frowned as other sounds emerged from the desert. Straining engines... wolf howls...

She shook her head. God, please. Not more foes to face.

Somehow, she couldn't bring herself to prepare. Instead, she hung on to Buck, leaving it to fate to kill her or send a huge stroke of luck her way. When canine pants and footfalls sounded all around, she kept her eyes closed. Buck raised his head and growled, but she didn't have it in her any more.

Vehicles squeaked to a halt at the foot of the bluff, and the sound of boots over dry terrain drew near. But it was only when a familiar voice called out that she finally opened her eyes.

She stared into the darkness. "Kyle?"

Shock gave way to relief and then to fear. She had a full-grown wolf in her lap. What if Kyle pulled a weapon and shot Buck?

But Kyle seemed perfectly at ease amid the pack of wolves that had appeared. He cocked his head, then nodded to her.

"Hi."

She nearly broke out in dazed laughter. Her duty partner was a man of few words, but *Hi* at a time like this?

Then Kyle addressed the wolf in her arms. "You okay, Roy?"

When Buck gave a weak wag of his tail, one of the wolves murmured, and Kyle nodded.

Andie stared. "You know this is Roy?"

Kyle nodded.

The overwhelmed gears in her mind turned, slowly making the connection. Kyle... Pack of wolves... All the rumors about Twin Moon Ranch...

She stared at her partner. Was Kyle a wolf too?

A woman stepped up beside Kyle, flashing a sympathetic smile. It was Stefanie, Kyle's partner.

"Are you really all right?" Stefanie asked. When Andie nodded, Stefanie crouched down, touching her shoulder. "Believe me, I know this is hard to process."

Andie nodded dumbly. That was for sure.

"I guess we have a lot to explain," Kyle added, though the way he rubbed his chin suggested he didn't know where to start.

And heck, neither did Andie. Somehow, she'd ended up on a bluff with a wolf and the body of a bizarre creature — a skinwalker? — lying somewhere nearby. Not exactly the kind of case she or Kyle could call in to headquarters.

Another man stepped up beside Kyle — a tall, brooding figure Andie recognized as Ty Hawthorne, head of Twin Moon Ranch.

"No time now. Not before we take care of all this," he growled, looking none too pleased as he glanced over the cliff.

Stefanie gave Andie an encouraging smile. "I promise, it will be all right. And as for explaining, well..." She grinned and shot Buck a wink. "Maybe we'll leave that to him."

Chapter Twenty-One

Up until the wolves of Twin Moon Ranch arrived, Roy had almost slipped into a state of bliss. His injuries burned, but that was balanced by the sheer joy of Andie holding him close. And not just that, but with Andie finally knowing about his two sides and accepting both.

But when howls and footfalls had heralded the arrival of the Twin Moon wolves, he'd tensed all over again. He'd chosen to leave the pack a long, long time ago. What would their reaction be?

He imagined the snarls and derision he would face. Something along the lines of *You left of your own free will, so why the hell are you back now?*

Sympathy would be even worse, with folks murmuring behind his back. *Poor guy. He always was a little messed up. After his brother died, and after all those years in wolf form... Well, he's got to be nuts.*

The hair on his back stood as they approached, though he didn't have the energy to creak to his feet. He just lay there, dreading what would happen next.

But it wasn't that way at all. No growls, no snickers. Just quiet chuffs of recognition and... respect?

The nearest wolf — one with bright blue eyes and a fair, gold-hued pelt who acted like he owned the place — crept up slowly, then sniffed the air and wagged its tail.

Roy?

Roy flicked an ear. Wait. Cody?

When Roy made a neutral huffing sound, the wolf broke into a huge canine grin.

Yep, that was Cody, all right. Happy-go-lucky Cody, who laughed and joked his way through life.

But something was different about him now. There was an air of authority about him, and a *don't fuck with me* attitude that said he'd risen to a high rank in the pack.

Roy sniffed again. Huh. Apparently, the ranch playboy had finally grown up.

Wow, Roy. So good to see you! Cody looked genuinely glad. *It's been a long time.*

Roy nodded wearily. Yes, it had been.

Another wolf approached, then another and another until it seemed like half the damn pack was there, sniffing curiously. On the outside, Roy was a rock, but inside, he cringed. So many packmates who knew too much about his past. So much shared history, not all of which was nice.

But Cody wasn't the only one to appear happy, even relieved to see him. A beautiful dark she-wolf — Cody's sister Tina — appeared and wagged her tail.

Roy! Roy! So good to see you back! Are you okay?

Roy! someone else called in delight. *It's Roy!*

That set everyone else into motion, and soon, they all swarmed around, nuzzling his shoulder or brushing him with wagging tails.

The pack must have grown in his absence, because there were a few wolves he didn't recognize, but the others soon filled them in.

It's Roy! He's back after so long! Hooray!

Tina even choked up a little, and damn. Roy nearly did too.

Way back, when he'd left, he'd simply slipped away one night, overwhelmed by emotions and dark memories. No one would miss him, and he wouldn't miss them. Such was the picture that he'd gradually cemented into his heart.

But their reactions painted a totally different image, and all the things he'd blotted out came rushing back. The friendly faces, not just the foes. The kindness. The sense of family. The community that had mourned the loss of one of their own.

Thank goodness you're all right. Thank goodness you've come back.

With every friendly word and enthusiastic tail wag, Roy's reservations faded. Maybe coming back wouldn't be so bad after all.

Then Ty Hawthorne, the pack alpha, prowled up in human form, making Roy tense all over again. The others parted like water before Moses, and Roy gulped, forcing his chin high.

Growing up, he and Ty had had a lot in common. Same age, same size — same lots of things, really, right down to the stubborn streak they both possessed. But Ty had grown up as the undisputed heir to the pack throne, while Roy had had to carve out his own tenuous niche.

The others might be warm and friendly, but Ty was rough. Gruff. A man of swift judgment and few words, like his authoritarian father had been.

Or maybe not, because a moment later, Ty broke into a wide grin.

"Good to see you, man. It's been too long."

Roy nearly flopped to the ground in shock.

A she-wolf trotted up beside Ty, rubbing along his legs the way only a mate would. Roy stared. Wow. Had she helped soften Ty up? Well, *soft* might not be the word, because a rock would always be a rock. But even granite could develop smoother edges over time.

Behind Ty, Tina grinned and sent a wry comment into his mind. *Sometimes, even people you're sure will never change actually change. Small miracle, in Ty's case, but true.* Then she chuckled. *You should see my dad.*

Roy must have winced, because Tina laughed. *Don't worry. Dad moved to Colorado. You'll find the ranch a little more easygoing these days.*

His heart raced — in a good way — at the thought.

"You okay?" Ty asked.

Roy took a deep breath, taking stock. His body ached, but he could feel his shifter healing slowly kick in. More importantly, Andie was all right — and okay with who he was.

And on top of all that, the pack was happy to see him rather than suspicious that he might have gone rogue, crazy, or schizophrenic. So, huh. Maybe his big mistake wasn't coming home, but in leaving in the first place.

Then again, he wasn't actually home yet. The bluff was on the outskirts of town and a few miles outside pack territory. Acceptance out here didn't mean he was welcome on the ranch. Plus, humans weren't welcome there, and he wasn't going anywhere without his mate.

Roy held his breath as Ty turned to Andie.

"You okay, miss?" Then Ty paused at a rumble from Kyle. "Officer, I mean?"

Shit, shit, shit. Roy tensed all over again. Andie embodied everything shifters feared being discovered by — humans and the law.

Andie's fingers remained tight in Roy's fur, but she nodded. "A little shell-shocked, but otherwise, I'm fine. Thanks."

Ty nodded, then looked around, grim. "What a mess."

But instead of snapping his fingers and ordering a couple of wolves to escort Andie away as Roy feared, Ty gestured to three other wolves. "You, you, and you — I need you to stay and clean up."

Each of the wolves confirmed with a low bark, impressing Roy all over again. Unlike his father, who'd led by brute power, Ty led through respect.

"Cody, you stay and take charge," Ty went on.

Cody gave a canine nod and strode over to the others to confer. So, whew. Roy's fears about humans discovering the grisly scene were eased.

Then Ty looked back at Roy and Andie, considering. Finally, he said, "We have a lot to discuss—"

But since it's so late... Tina butted in, giving her brother a firm look.

Ty frowned, then nodded. "I suppose it can wait." He paused there, fixing Andie with that alpha gaze of his. "But we'd appreciate you keeping quiet about all this until we've had a chance to discuss it."

Roy had seen dozens of tough shifters wither under Ty's laser gaze, but Andie only gulped.

"I'm not sure what I would say, so yes. I'll wait until you've had a chance to...um...explain." Her eyes swept over the bluff, the pack of wolves, and finally, Roy.

He swallowed hard. Yeah, he had a hell of a lot to explain. But right now...

Ty must have read his mind, because he softened a little and asked Andie, "Would you like a ride?"

Roy frowned. A ride where? Andie had somehow kept herself together throughout it all. But bringing her to the heart of a wolf pack was not what she needed right now.

Tina bumped Ty's leg, making him frown and listen to whatever his sister communicated next. Then he nodded slowly and looked back at Andie.

"Like I said, we can give you a ride — any place you'd like to go. Cody can bring your car later."

Andie exhaled in relief, looked at Roy, and then nodded. "My place would be great. Thank you."

Chapter Twenty-Two

And so it was that Roy spent the second night of his life in Andie's bed — and the third, and the fourth, and many, many more. A whole, peaceful week of quiet days and blissful nights, interrupted only by two short visits.

Kyle was the first to come by, the morning after the fight. He'd already checked on Yvette, who was fine, if overexcited. She was convinced Stanton had murdered Brady, and that he was a skinwalker. But since she hadn't actually seen him shift... Kyle managed to convince her not to share that story with the police or anyone else.

A friend of a friend put me in touch with Stanton, she'd told Kyle. *He sounded like the right man to scare people away and stop the Lazy Q from getting ripped apart by developers. But, hell. I guess I'd better not tell that to the police.*

Kyle winked at Andie in recalling that part. *I think that's best,* was all he'd said to Yvette. So, whew. That base was covered.

Kyle also filled in Roy's spotty memories of Stanton with information he'd gleaned on Twin Moon Ranch.

Apparently, the guy really looked up to you, Kyle said, shocking Roy. *After you left, he kept talking about leaving everything behind to go back to nature. In the end, he was kicked off the ranch, and what he got up to... Well, he might have meant well, but the way he went about it...* Kyle shook his head.

In a way, Roy felt sorry for Stanton, knowing firsthand how hard it was to escape a troubled past. He'd felt like an outsider for most of his life, but Stanton had it worse with his unusual, mixed shifter side.

No one on the ranch understood why he hid it, Kyle lamented. *They would have accepted it if they knew.*

That, Roy wasn't so sure about — not the way things used to be at the ranch.

But anyway, it was hard to muster much sympathy for such a ruthless man.

Definitely one of the hopeless cases, as Andie had said.

Kyle had also told police headquarters Andie had come down with a debilitating flu and needed a few days to recover.

"They said to stay home and make sure you don't infect everyone else." Kyle grinned.

When Roy had first met Kyle, he wasn't so sure about the guy. But now, he could see that Andie's trust in Kyle was well placed.

And thank goodness, because that went a long way in helping Andie come to grips with the shifter world. Kyle's calm, *everything will be okay* demeanor made the information that much easier to digest, and his law enforcement perspective resonated with Andie too.

In the end, Kyle stayed for hours, eventually joined by his mate, Stefanie. Both had been turned shifter as adults, which also helped reassure Andie about their kind.

The second visit had been from Ty, Lana, and Tina — the leading wolves of Twin Moon Ranch. A catch-up chat, as Tina put it, in which Roy and Andie shared everything they'd observed about Stanton and Lazy Q Ranch.

Andie had been a little shaky — not that she showed it much — at the prospect of a visit by three more people who could turn into wolves, but Lana and Tina had done as much as Kyle to put her at ease.

Every human has an animal side, Tina had said, then winked. *Haven't you ever looked up at the full moon and wanted to howl in glee?*

Andie had broken into a smile at that, and Roy thought about all the times she'd sat on her boulder, gazing at the stars and moon.

I guess I have, Andie admitted. *More often than I wanted to acknowledge, maybe.*

So, whew. Interactions like that helped normalize the prospect of a shifter world.

By the time they stood to leave, Ty seemed satisfied that all loose ends had been accounted for — except one.

"Now, we just have to worry about what happens next with Lazy Q Ranch," he'd sighed.

But Lana, Ty's mate, had nodded slyly. "Let me get to work on that."

Roy wasn't sure what Lana had in mind, but he wasn't about to ask.

Otherwise, Roy and Andie had been left to themselves. Well, a handful of wolves from Twin Moon Ranch had stuck around to guard the area, just in case, but they kept their distance. The same went for the police who passed through the area, investigating the unsolved mystery of Brady's murder — and the still-missing cassowary.

But all in all, a feeling of peace had settled over Andie's little corner of paradise, and that was enough for Roy. Finally, he'd found a place where he fit in.

He didn't have to force himself into life on the ranch or life in the wild. He could live with the right amount of distance to each.

And zero distance to our mate, his wolf chuckled.

He held her tightly, and she held him. They spent hours talking, explaining so much. The past. The present. Their hopes for the future.

Andie had made him shift in and out of wolf form several times, and she stood shaking her head each time.

"Amazing," she said one time.

"Incredible," she'd whispered after another.

But the time Roy would keep etched in his heart forever was when she'd knelt to stroke his fur, thrown her arms around his neck, mumbling, "God, I missed you, Buck."

They'd stayed like that a long time, eyes closed, hearts full.

Then Andie had looked deep into his eyes and made the moment even more memorable. "I missed both of you. I mean, whenever you were gone." She gulped, then buried her face in his fur. "Somehow, deep down, I knew. I knew you were Buck, and Buck was you."

I knew too, he'd replied, at least in snuffly wolf talk. *I knew you were my destined mate.*

Explaining mates proved to be the trickiest part. Because how and when was a guy supposed to blurt something like that out?

Finally, he found his chance one night. They'd gone to bed a little slow and shy, only to rush headlong into reckless, panting, full speed ahead passion when a few light kisses turned into raging need neither could resist.

"Is this a wolf thing?" Andie broke out of a deep kiss long enough to claw the clothes off his body. "I mean, is that what makes me feel like I'll die if I don't have you?"

He'd stopped long enough to stare into her eyes and whisper, "It's because we're mates. We're destined for each other."

He didn't say more just then, too busy stripping her out of the rest of her clothes. Then he got a little sidetracked by kisses that took him from her mouth to her breasts and farther south. And after that, well, he couldn't think straight, not with Andie guiding his head to her core, where he proceeded to lick them both into a wild, heaving orgasm.

It was only after that, when they'd both lain panting and sweating, that he got himself together enough to explain about mates, instincts, and sacred bonds that lasted forever.

"A mating bite?" Andie had gone a little wide-eyed at that part.

They hadn't been intimate long enough for him to know all her preferences, but he knew enough to tell that kink wasn't her thing.

But a moment later, her eyes sparkled, and like so much else about the shifter world, she accepted it with surprising calm, as if it were all encoded in her DNA and only rushing to the surface now. So maybe Tina was right — every human had an animal side, ready to be awakened in the right circumstances.

"A bite...where?" Her voice went a little husky as she ran her hands over his body.

Her lips followed soon after, and all Roy could do was lie back and mumble.

"Here?" She kissed his ear while circling his nipple with a finger.

"Close," he choked out.

She grinned and wrapped her fingers around his hard shaft. "Here?"

He threw his head back while she stroked up and down, then murmured, "No biting there, lady. But please... Don't stop."

She chuckled and shuffled lower... lower...

His lips moved silently when she sucked him in, transporting him to the edge of heaven.

"So good," she murmured after a few more slides. "But back to biting..." She crawled back up his body, kissed his mouth hard, then drew back. "Maybe you should just show me."

Roy's wolf howled, and it took everything he had not to rush.

"Well, you start like this..." he whispered, easing down over her body. Easing *into* her body, slowly at first, then deeper. Soon, they were rocking in perfect time and mumbling in sheer ecstasy.

Andie tipped her head back, exposing her throat, as if she already knew where the bite would go and how good it would feel.

Just in case, Roy paused long enough to whisper, "Biting means forever. You can't change your mind after."

"I want forever," she panted, bucking up into him. "I want you. Please..."

Her motion set him off again, and he closed his eyes, focusing intently.

Yes, his wolf hissed as his canines extended.

He bent, nuzzling her neck while keeping up the steady rhythm.

"Yes..." Andie moaned, pulling him closer.

Instinct was an amazing thing, Roy figured. Instinct and destiny, guiding each of them.

Her pulse bumped under his lips, and sweat glazed her skin. When he scraped his teeth over the right spot, they both groaned. A moment later, when he bit down, slow but steady and ever deeper, they both cried out.

Andie tightened her legs around his waist, reminding him to keep moving there. *I need you... Want you... Forever...*

Clear as a bell, her voice filtered into his mind, driving him wild. She was his. He was hers. They were forever connected.

Need you, he whispered back. *Want you. Forever.*

Her life's blood swirled a cell's width away from his canines. With one final, mind-blurring effort, he pushed his teeth deeper and thrust even harder. Then, with a keening cry, they both came. Soft, radiant light flooded Roy's mind, blinding him to everything but the ecstasy of the moment. Andie moaned, lost in the same blissful sensation.

Eventually, Roy found himself floating back to his senses, more a witness to his body than its master. He felt his canines recede and his tongue press down over the wound on Andie's neck until the skin healed. Then he slumped over her, pressing her into the mattress.

Andie patted his back for a long time before whispering in wonder, "I can see myself, but in your mind."

He rolled to lie by her side, keeping nice and close. "That's how it is with mates. The special connection."

See? he added a moment later, speaking directly into her mind.

See how much I love you? his wolf added.

Andie laughed out loud and stroked around his ear, just the way the wolf liked. "Yes, I see you too." Then she paused, cupped his face, and spoke into his mind. *So, you can tell how good I feel?*

Roy grinned. That must be it — the pinnacle of his life. His whole being pulsed with joy and satisfaction. The funny thing was, he'd felt that a moment earlier, and just before that, and earlier still. So maybe life didn't have a single, bright peak. Maybe happiness could linger on and on. Maybe even for a lifetime.

He nodded, then kissed her. *Yes, I can tell. But you know what?*

He slid a hand along her smooth, soft skin, aroused all over again.

What? Her eyes sparkled as she drew her leg along his.

I think I can make you feel even better. He cupped her breast, drawing a finger around the nipple.

She pulled him closer. *Not sure we can top that bite, but I'm willing to try.*

He grinned. *It's not a one-time deal, you know. We can do it again...* He ducked to kiss her neck as another wave of heat pulsed through his body. *And again...*

Andie answered with the last coherent word either of them spoke for a while. For nearly the whole night, it seemed, as they kept coming together in unfettered passion.

Again and again. I like the sound of that.

Epilogue

Three months later...

Andie pushed the door of her squad car closed and headed for headquarters, converging with Officers Chavez and Lee. Kyle was half a step ahead of her, eager to get home to his mate. An idea Andie could identify with, being a happily mated shifter herself.

She hid a little grin. Funny, how much life could change.

Lee sighed. "Another long day, but at least it was a halfway normal one."

Andie nodded in agreement. She never thought burglary, a road closure, and a drunk driver arrest — before anyone was hurt, thank goodness — would strike her as normal. But it sure beat the days she'd endured a few months back.

"I don't know," Chavez joked. "I kind of miss all that skinwalker action."

Lee shook his head. "There was no skinwalker action, remember? It turned out to be Big Bird after all."

Andie kept her mouth shut. That wasn't exactly the truth, but that was one of many lessons she'd learned in the past few months.

Let sleeping dogs lie, Kyle murmured into her mind.

No one had taught her as much about the shifter world as Roy, but Kyle had been a godsend when it came to learning to toe the line between the human and shifter worlds — especially as a police officer.

So she didn't say a word. If humans believed the cassowary was to blame for the string of bloody attacks, so be it. Humans could sleep better that way, and shifters could too, without fear of humans snooping around in search of the supernatural.

Plus, there was a certain neatness to it all. The escaped cassowary might not have killed Brady, but it did threaten another rancher a week after the murder. The bird had come within an inch of slicing the man down the chest. Luckily, the man's girlfriend was a quick draw and had gunned the bird down, thus ending skinwalker speculation for good.

Well, a few, like Yvette, still believed. But the press — along with most of the public — had long since moved on to fresh stories, like a spectacular drug bust in a former judge's home.

Chavez chuckled. "We can always hope for that ghost in the old copper mine to start haunting again."

Everyone laughed as they went about their end-of-shift routines — turning in their gear, signing off on the day's reports, and trading uniform jackets for civilian wear. Andie did it all in double time.

"Wow. Someone's in a rush tonight," Chavez teased as Andie headed for the door. "You got a hot date?"

Andie threw him a look but didn't slow down. Yes, she did, as a matter of fact — if dates included going for a run under the full moon in wolf form.

Lee laughed. "Andie has a hot date every night these days. She and that new man of hers. She's almost as bad as Kyle when he first met Stefanie."

Andie laughed. If only they knew about the power of shifter love.

And, ha — that meant her. A shifter! Even after three months, the realization still struck her. But it was just as Tina had said — her second side had emerged slowly and naturally, the way some folks developed a new phase or interest. Not that shifting was like taking up yoga or watercoloring, but heck. It hadn't been as startling a change as she'd imagined.

"Don't go knocking true love," Kyle growled back.

He winked, then whispered into her mind as all packmates could.

Full moon tonight. See you and Roy soon?

See you soon, she whispered back, then waved to the others. "Bye, guys. Be good."

"Ha," Chavez laughed. "While you're busy being bad, you mean?"

Andie decided not to grace that with a comment. By the time she stepped out the door, Chavez was on to a fresh topic anyway.

"Well, I guess it's time for me to check in with the chief. Maybe I'll finally get that promotion I deserve."

"And maybe I'll win the state lottery," Lee sighed.

Andie chuckled all the way to her car. Some things never changed, and that was comforting, considering all the changes in her private life.

She drove home as fast as the speed limit allowed, only slowing when asphalt petered out to dirt road. Along the way, she soaked in the beauty of it all. The stunning sunset colors. The first spring shoots emerging along the sides of the road. Bats flitting over majestic cottonwoods that followed the curving path of a creek.

God, she loved Arizona. The delicate details, the grand mesas. The subtle seasons. But most of all...

I love my mate, her inner wolf chimed in. *So, hurry up.*

Hearing her animal side seemed totally natural these days too. It was just like the self-talk she'd engaged in all her life, only in a deeper, more direct tone — and a little naughtier.

Her heart rose as she came to the overlook onto her home valley. The lights were on over at Lazy Q Ranch, where an amiable, hardworking new manager had moved in. A she-wolf and mother of two, MaryLynn had been brought in by the new owners — the wolves of Twin Moon Ranch.

Financially, it's a stretch, Tina Hawthorne had said two months back, *but I think it will be worth it. The bigger buffer we have to the outer world, the better.*

Jose had been coaxed back to work too, and Andie loved seeing him pass by on his palomino, herding the goats with Lucky.

Having MaryLynn as general manager and her bear shifter mate as grounds keeper made for two huge improvements over the old management. Best of all, Roy was the new head of security at Lazy Q Ranch. The perfect job that let him spend his days roving the desert in human or wolf form.

Some evenings, he spent at the Lone Wolf, as Andie still did. She loved walking in and spotting him there, playing checkers with Mick. So much, she usually paused at the door just to watch them.

Rita would do the same from behind the bar, beaming at the two of them.

It's just like my dad always said, Andie had once confided in Rita. *Proof that for all the cruelty in the world, there's good too. Happiness. Love. Laughter.*

She could picture them now — Roy moving a piece for Mick, then considering his own move — all the while minding the crowd. The moment a customer got the slightest bit rowdy, Roy would bristle, glare, or grumble. And just like that, the perpetrator would pale and settle down.

It's handy, having you two around, Rita had once said.

Andie had grinned back. *It's handy, having a place to hang out. Otherwise, we'd never get out.*

It was true. Neither she nor Roy was very social, but the Lone Wolf kept them in touch with the human world in a way that suited them both.

Inevitably, evenings there would end with Andie announcing something like, *Well, I hate to drag Roy away, but...*

Her wolf would chuckle quietly and add, *But I really need to get him home and naked.*

A sentiment flaring in her right now, knowing Roy was already home and waiting.

She took a hard right onto the half-mile-long track that served as her driveway, nearly home. And a good thing, too, because the sun had just dipped below the horizon. She parked and rushed inside.

"Roy?"

Her voice echoed through silence, but that didn't worry her. She stepped through the empty house, shedding clothes as she went. Off with her jacket, sweater, and shirt. Off with her boots and pants.

She dropped her socks on the back porch, then continued out into the desert in nothing but underwear and a pair of flip-flops. Her skin was covered with goose bumps, but that had more to do with the thrill of anticipation than the cool spring air. She tipped her head up at the first, faint stars before continuing to her special boulder.

"Buck?" she whispered into the night.

Yes, she still thought of her mate as Buck when he was in wolf form and Roy as a human. That was the way she'd first gotten to know her mate, and hey, it worked for them both.

"Are you out there?" She smiled, knowing he was. She could sense her mate anywhere, the same way he could sense her.

Her pulse revved a little higher, and her smile stretched. The bushes rustled, though Buck didn't emerge.

"Such a tease." She sighed. "Well, two can play that game." She reached around to unclip her bra and slowly, sensually slid it off. She dropped it to the boulder, then hooked her thumbs into the sides of her panties and worked them down with an extra wiggle of her hips.

The bushes were perfectly still, and she could sense Buck staring.

Tossing the panties aside, she rubbed her arms. "A little chilly out here."

Chilly enough to make her nipples peak — or was that her libido at work?

Not chilly at all, her wolf murmured. *Pretty warm, in fact.*

Raging hot was more like it, especially once Buck prowled into sight and circled the boulder, swishing his tail.

This woman is mine, his movements declared. *This territory is mine. Be in no doubt about that, world.*

"So there you are," she murmured, letting him stake his claim. That was one of those canine instincts she'd come to recognize. And, hell. She would be staking her claim to him the moment she shifted to wolf form, rubbing along his body in long, hard strokes.

Long... Hard... Her wolf giggled.

As if she wasn't already aroused after a long day way from her mate.

"So, what will it be?" She gazed down at him. "Option A or B?"

The mental pictures she sent into his mind filled in the details. In Option A, they were naked, sweaty, and human, shagging to high heaven right there on that rock. In Option B, they were loping to a mesa in wolf form, then howling to the full moon under the starlight. A human might not get the appeal of that, but her wolf side was genuinely torn.

"Why not both?" Roy replied in a husky voice. He'd shifted in the blink of an eye, leaving a slight shimmer in the air as he straightened to his full height.

Chiseled abs and biceps rippled as Roy scaled the rock. The moment he drew close, Andie wrapped her arms around him.

"I suppose we could give the moon a little more time to rise."

With that, she dove into a deep, hungry kiss. Within minutes, they were both horizontal on that bed of a boulder, limbs and lips intertwined.

"Yes..." Andie moaned as he slid deep inside.

Soon, she was moving in time with his body, taking him deeper every time. Around her, the sky, stars, and stunning landscape blurred. Her world shrank down to her body, his, and the raging, inner need.

Mate, her wolf side groaned in a mix of pleasure and greed. *More. Please...*

His scent intoxicated her, making her cry for more...more...

She shuddered and came, gasping and gripping Roy's shoulders hard.

Roy had his head back and his teeth bared, equally engulfed by ecstasy.

Eventually, the stars came back into focus, along with the sounds of the desert at night. As Roy lay down beside her, the moon rose, casting them both in its pure, pale light.

Andie patted Roy, then chuckled, making him look up.
"What?"

She laughed. "I want it all. You. This. That run to the mesa..."

He grinned. "Welcome to the life of a shifter."

They lay there for few blissful minutes before finally stirring and sliding to the ground.

"After you." Roy motioned.

Andie hid a smile. Roy had a penchant for watching her. And honestly, she loved the way it made her feel. Beautiful. Sexy. Desired. All those things that had no place in her day job.

Slowly, she sank to all fours, closing her eyes. Picturing longer ears and a tail, she wiggled her hips, then inhaled. Moonlight washed over her, coaxing her animal side out, while allowing her human side to recede.

When she blinked and stretched again, it was in wolf form, with her shoulders low and her tail up high. She paused for a moment, still amazed that was really her. Then she stuck out her nose and indulged in a hefty shake that started at the tip of her soft nose and traveled all the way to her tail.

Roy followed suit, and they spent a full minute brushing against each other in long, possessive strokes.

Mine, his wolf declared again and again.

No, mine. She ducked under the coarse fur of his neck and flicked her tail.

Then they were off, loping easily along. The ground blurred under her paws, together with all the scents assaulting her sensitive nose — sage, heather, and the sweet odor of prickly pear. To her canine vision, the desert was a dramatic film noir of blacks, whites, and grays, emphasizing the sharp lines of the mesa. At the top, they stood still, taking in what felt like a kingdom of their own.

But not only their own, as the sonorous howls that rose all around reminded them. Andie loved living in her own space, and Roy did too. But at the same time, they were part of a patchwork connected by a powerful pack bond, from Twin Moon Ranch to Lazy Q and all the way over to Tina Hawthorne-Rivera's home on Seymour Ranch.

Andie marveled at the extent of the secret world she'd been lucky enough to join.

Roy bumped her impatiently. *Ready?*

She grinned. In their early days as part of Twin Moon pack, Roy had been content to howl from the mesa, apart from the rest. But these days...

Ready.

The moment she said it, they both took off, zigzagging down the other side of the mesa. Once they reached the valley floor, they accelerated until reaching a hollow where gleeful yips broke out all around.

Roy! Andie! So nice you could make it!

Wouldn't miss it, Roy assured them with a hearty chuff.

His mother wasn't one of them since she'd left the ranch a few years after he had. Apparently, she was doing well in New Mexico, and Andie and Roy were planning to visit... eventually. For now, though, their hearts and minds were firmly in the present.

Andie yipped as two wolves rushed to greet her and Roy with canine sniffs and wagging tails. Cody and Roy immediately broke into a gleeful play-wrestle, rearing up on their hind legs and snapping at thin air.

Heather laughed. *Boys, boys.*

They broke apart with a laughing yip and rejoined their mates just as Kyle and Stefanie trotted up.

Hi, you two, Stefanie called.

Kyle shot Andie a rueful grin, which she returned. They'd always gotten along well at work, but a wall had always separated them as far as off-duty time went. Now, as packmates, that was gone, and Kyle and Stefanie had become their closest friends.

They all came together in a happy huddle, yipping joyously.

You again, Kyle joked.

Andie laughed. Yes, her again. But a freer, more easygoing version than she got to show at work.

A deep chuff sounded, making everyone look up. Ty, the pack alpha, surveyed the scene from a rocky outcrop. Beside him, Lana wagged her tail.

Andie yipped in greeting, while Roy dipped his chin in a sign of respect. Ty wasn't big on protocol — thank goodness, because Andie had heard the stories about his father, the previous alpha — but it was hard not to respond to that sense of authority he exuded.

Hi, everyone! Lana called, making sure to keep things light. *Rae and Zack should be here soon.*

Andie wagged her tail eagerly, then laughed at herself. If anyone had told her she would one day be a wolf shifter and excited about things like running under the full moon with Rae, the pack's legendary Mistress of the Hunt, Andie would have called them crazy. But here she was, loving every minute of her new life.

One by one or in pairs, the rest of the pack appeared. Tina and Rick loped up from the direction of Seymour Ranch, a little out of breath.

Sorry. Aunt Jean is babysitting, but she was running a little late, Tina explained with a smile.

Rick puffed out his chest a little, as if their baby girl was the most priceless addition to the pack.

A good thing there wasn't a contest for proud dads, because Cody, Ty, and Kyle were just as bad.

The ground rumbled with heavy hoofbeats as Axel, the massive boar shifter, appeared next with Beth, his mate, smiling beside him.

Hello, everyone, the she-wolf murmured as Axel dragged a hoof through the dirt. They were both a little shy, though both could be ferocious in defense of their pack.

Everyone milled around, chatting in excitement. The pack gathered regularly, but never with as much anticipation as on full-moon nights. When Rae and Zack trotted into view, a cacophony of happy barks and impatient yips broke out.

Rae made a quick round of those gathered, then sat in the center of the clearing and looked up at Ty. An expectant hush fell over everyone, and Andie's heart thumped. She leaned into Roy.

I love this part. Where would I be if you hadn't helped me become part of this pack?

He rubbed his chin over her neck. *I love this too. And where would I be if you hadn't helped me?*

Everyone waited as Ty took a deep breath, raised his muzzle, and let out a long, warbling howl. When he broke off, the only sound in the air was his own echo. When Ty inhaled for a longer, second howl, Lana joined him, as did the others, one by one.

Roy lifted his muzzle and howled, joining the others.

Arrroooo…

As a human, Andie might have found the sound sad. And some howls could be, but not most, and not this one. Roy's was a song of joy and belonging. Of love, hope, and home.

Andie took a deep breath, then joined in the song.

Arrroooo, her higher, smoother voice joined Roy's and the others'. All around her, the notes wove together, wrapping around her and Roy. Telling them *We are all in this together. We all belong.*

Andie leaned into her mate, sending her song to the sky, to the stars, to the moon.

For years, she'd felt something was missing. Now, all those empty spaces had been filled.

Thanks to you, she whispered into her true love's mind.

Roy dipped his head before continuing his grateful tune.

No. Thanks to you, my mate.

Sneak Peek: Damnation: the She-Wolf's Forbidden Alpha Grizzly

He hasn't forgotten her, and she sure hasn't forgiven him.

Jessica Macks is a she-wolf on the run from a band of murderous rogues. When she finds a job at a shifter bar, it seems like a safe haven from her hunted life on the road. But the minute she walks through the swinging doors of the Blue Moon Saloon and comes face-to-face with the man she once loved, she's tempted to march right back out. No way, no how is she risking her heart to that infuriating alpha bear again.

Simon Voss thought he lost everything in an ambush months before: his home, his family, his past. His new job at the Blue Moon Saloon is a desperately needed fresh start on life. Then along comes Jessica, the irresistible she-wolf his clan forced him to reject years before. When Simon is obliged to hire Jessica and work side by side with the one woman to ever make his bear go wild, he's half in heaven, half in hell. He hasn't forgotten her, and she sure as hell hasn't forgiven him. Is this just another path to heartbreak or his last chance to claim his destined mate?

Books by Anna Lowe

The Wolves of Twin Moon Ranch

Desert Hunt (the Prequel)

Desert Moon (Book 1)

Desert Blood (Book 2)

Desert Fate (Book 3)

Desert Heart (Book 4)

Desert Rose (Book 5)

Desert Roots (Book 6)

Desert Destiny (Book 7)

Sasquatch Surprise (Book 8)

Desert Yule (a short story)

Desert Wolf: Complete Collection (Four short stories)

Aloha Shifters - Jewels of the Heart

Lure of the Dragon (Book 1)

Lure of the Wolf (Book 2)

Lure of the Bear (Book 3)

Lure of the Tiger (Book 4)

Love of the Dragon (Book 5)

Lure of the Fox (Book 6)

Aloha Shifters - Pearls of Desire

Rebel Dragon (Book 1)

Rebel Bear (Book 2)

Rebel Lion (Book 3)

Rebel Wolf (Book 4)

Rebel Heart (A prequel to Book 5)

Rebel Alpha (Book 5)

Fire Maidens - Billionaires & Bodyguards

Fire Maidens: Paris (Book 1)

Fire Maidens: London (Book 2)

Fire Maidens: Rome (Book 3)

Fire Maidens: Portugal (Book 4)

Fire Maidens: Ireland (Book 5)

Fire Maidens: Scotland (Book 6)

Fire Maidens: Venice (Book 7)

Fire Maidens: Greece (Book 8)

Fire Maidens: Switzerland (Book 9)

Blue Moon Saloon

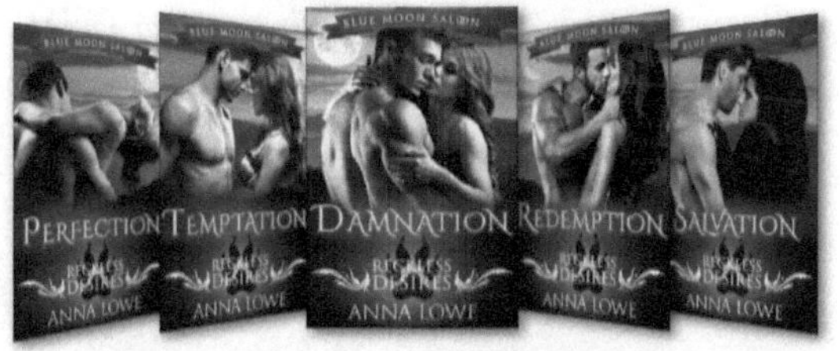

Perfection (a short story prequel)

Damnation (Book 1)

Temptation (Book 2)

Redemption (Book 3)

Salvation (Book 4)

Deception (Book 5)

Celebration (a holiday treat)

Shifters in Vegas

Paranormal romance with a zany twist

Gambling on Trouble

Gambling on Her Dragon

Gambling on Her Bear

Gambling on Her Panther

Serendipity Adventure Romance

Off the Charts

Uncharted

Entangled

Windswept

Adrift

Travel Romance

Veiled Fantasies

Island Fantasies

www.annalowebooks.com

About the Author

USA Today and Amazon bestselling author Anna Lowe loves putting the "hero" back into heroine and letting location ignite a passionate romance. She likes a heroine who is independent, intelligent, and imperfect – a woman who is doing just fine on her own. But give the heroine a good man – not to mention a chance to overcome her own inhibitions – and she'll never turn down the chance for adventure, nor shy away from danger.

Anna loves dogs, sports, and travel – and letting those inspire her fiction. On any given weekend, you might find her hiking in the mountains or hunched over her laptop, working on her latest story. Either way, the day will end with a chunk of dark chocolate and a good read.

Visit AnnaLoweBooks.com